D1093986

Pendragon

fin la marche de gaule & la pe tite bretaigne auoit .ii. rois an chienement qui eftoient frere g maimz. lanoient .ii. fereurs ger maines lunus ...

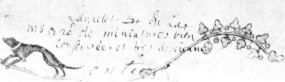

Pendragon

ARTHUR AND HIS BRITAIN

JOSEPH P. CLANCY

PRAEGER PUBLISHERS

New York · Washington · London

The illustrations accompanying this text are from a manuscript of *Lancelot du Lac* written and illuminated in northeastern France at the beginning of the fourteenth century and now M. 805-6 in the Pierpont Morgan Library, New York. Reproduced with their permission are folios 1, 125, 170, 161, 24v, 166 and 38v.

Permission to reprint excerpts from the following works is gratefully acknowledged:
The Battle of Maldon, translated by Kevin Crossley-Holland, St. Martin's Press, 1965.
Beowulf, translated by Kevin Crossley-Holland, Farrar, Straus and Giroux, 1968.
The Earliest Welsh Poetry, translated by Joseph P. Clancy, St. Martin's Press, 1970.
Sir Gawain and the Green Knight, translated by Brian Stone, Penguin Books Ltd., 1959.

PRAEGER PUBLISHERS
111 Fourth Avenue, New York, N.Y. 10003, U.S.A.
5, Cromwell Place, London S.W.7, England

Published in the United States of America in 1971
by Praeger Publishers, Inc.

Printed in the United States of America

For Robert K. Windbiel and Donald F. Hayes,

Historians

Contents

Maps

Pendragon

1

Tellers of Tales:
The Poet and the Historian

The Poet says, "Once upon a time." The Historian says, "In A.D. 603." The Poet says, "At the splendid court of Camelot." The Historian says, "If there really was a Camelot, it may have been at Winchester, or perhaps at South Cadbury, but we do not know." The Poet says, "I shall tell you an exciting story." The Historian says, "I shall tell you a true story." Many of us, having spent our early years in the entertaining presence of the Poet, find the Historian rather dull company and avoid him whenever possible.

It was the Poet, I imagine, who first introduced you to Arthur—whether in the film *Camelot*, or in Tennyson's *Idylls of the King*, or in one of the many modern books that retell Sir Thomas Malory's *Morte d'Arthur*. (My own introduction came when, as a boy, I read Howard Pyle's version of the story.) That is not surprising: for a thousand years or so, Arthur has been in the hands of the Poet. Until fairly recently, the Historian wanted nothing to do with him—although it was a historian, William of Malmesbury, who in 1125 declared that Arthur should not "be dreamed of in false tales, but proclaimed in truthful histories." Since 1125 there have been many highly imaginative tales, very few truthful histories. And for good reasons.

"With a tale," Sir Philip Sidney wrote long ago, the Poet "cometh unto you, with a tale which holdeth children from play, and old men from the chimney corner." The Historian, wrote Sir Philip unkindly—he was, we must remember, himself a poet—the

3

Historian comes "laden with old mouse-eaten records, authorizing himself for the most part upon other histories, whose greatest authorities are built upon the notable foundation of hearsay; having much ado to accord differing writers and to pick truth out of partiality." In the case of Arthur, the Historian has all too few "mouse-eaten records," all too much "hearsay," and great difficulty bringing conflicting writers into accord. No wonder he has tended to give it up as an impossible job and let the Poet go on telling his fascinating tales, creating that "golden world" that, as Sidney rightly says, only the Poet can give us.

The golden world of King Arthur and Camelot lives, and will continue to live, in our imagination, whatever the Historian may do. The Historian himself can enjoy it thoroughly. But he is teased by questions: Was there really an Arthur? What was his world really like? To which the ordinary reader, you and I, may well ask in return: What does it matter?

If I thought it did not matter, that whatever truth can be found about Arthur and his Britain is so unimportant that it can interest only the most fact-obsessed historians, I should never have written this book. For I am by profession a poet, not a historian; it was not until many years after I had graduated from college that I was able to read a work of history with pleasure. That I am now, to my own surprise, attempting to write history comes from discovering that the truth about Arthur's Britain is as exciting as any poet's tales, that what Arthur did, in fact not in fiction, made a difference in men's lives for centuries after him. Arthur, in short, matters.

                    *   *   *   *   *

Let me confess: I have, to make a point, been treating the Poet and the Historian as opposing kinds of writers, each mistrustful of the other. It is not that simple. The Poet is interested in history: it gives him the raw materials, the people and the events, from which he makes his imaginary worlds, and those worlds, when he chooses, can mirror very closely the real world of history. There is a bit of the Historian in every poet, though more in some than in others. And there is a bit of the Poet in every historian, though again more in some than in others. It is not enough for the Historian to record the past: he should imagine it, re-create it for the reader. Where there are gaps in his knowledge, he will envy the Poet's freedom

THE PIERPONT MORGAN LIBRARY

to make things up, but he can and should use his imagination to construct, as far as the facts allow him, a probable version of how things really happened.

In dealing with Arthur and his Britain, the Historian needs to have a good deal of the Poet in him. The centuries from A.D. 400 to 600 are usually called "the Dark Ages in Britain"; whether or not they seemed dark to the men who lived at that time, they are dark indeed to those who wish to know how those men lived and what they did. We have very few written records of this era, and those we have are not always reliable.

Our chief source of knowledge for the major events of these centuries, for example, is a work by a monk named Gildas, who was born about A.D. 500 in western Britain. At some time between 540 and 547 he wrote a book called *De Excidio Britanniae* (*Concerning the Ruin of Britain*), which refers to events during the fifth and early sixth centuries in the course of denouncing the corrupt behavior of the people, especially the rulers, of Gildas' own time.

As a result, we are in the position of a man in the thirty-fifth century trying to learn about the war in Vietnam by reading a book that denounces American morals in the 1960's.

There are other books that deal with these centuries, but they cause at least as many problems as Gildas. Nennius, a ninth-century Welsh priest, produced a *Historia Brittonum,* making what he himself calls "a heap of all that I have found." One modern historian has said that we should be thankful for Nennius' "ignorance and his stupidity": because of these, his "heap," compiled four centuries after the events, contains bits and pieces that seem to come from Arthur's own time. Another important book is the *Anglo-Saxon Chronicle.* This is valuable for preserving some kind of record of the Saxon settlement in England, but it was composed, like Nennius' work, centuries later, and it shows more concern with giving a favorable picture of Saxon achievements than with historical accuracy. The most important thing about the *Chronicle,* for our purposes, is what it does *not* say. By its very silence, it testifies to a long period in which the Saxon advance was not only halted but turned back, and that is exactly the period in which, says Gildas, the Britons won a decisive victory under, says Nennius, the leadership of Arthur.

A historian, luckily, has sources of information other than books. He is helped greatly by the work of archaeologists: from the study of unearthed statues, weapons, and pottery, of excavated towns, fortresses, and farmhouses, some light is thrown upon these dark ages. But you can see that a historian needs to use his imagination to make a probable picture out of such fragments of evidence.

Take, most importantly, Arthur himself. It may surprise you to learn that there is no reference to Arthur from his own time, and that Gildas, writing of battles later connected with Arthur, never mentions him. Did he ever, the Historian naturally asks, really exist? But a British poet, Aneirin, in a work composed in about 595, praises a young warrior as heroic "even though he was not an Arthur." Aneirin throws this in as an offhand remark, assuming that of course everybody knows who Arthur was. And then there is the remarkable fact that Arthur's name, which had never appeared before among the British, is suddenly given to their sons by several British rulers in the late sixth and early seventh centuries. It is not unreasonable, therefore, to believe that an extraordinary man, one who could be used to measure other men's heroism, whose name would honor and inspire a child, actually lived in the early sixth century.

"It is not unreasonable to believe"—there speaks the Historian! Consider yourself warned: I shall use "perhaps" and "possibly" and "probably" quite often in the course of this book, more often than you (or I) would wish. Most of the book, to be frank, is one large *maybe*. I try to be cautious, but I often have to take risks: as an archaeologist reconstructs from ruins a model of how an original castle looked, so I reconstruct from facts and guesses a version of Arthur and his Britain, one that seems to me and to others possible and even probable. But I cannot prove that this is the way things really were. In one year, or ten, or twenty, documents may be found or buried evidence uncovered that will prove that I am often wrong—or, I like to think, that I am mostly right. I promise to make it clear when I am giving you facts and when I am dealing in "maybe's."

In shaping my reconstruction, I have drawn on a wide variety of materials, not only the books and archaeological discoveries I mentioned before, but also, for example, Welsh and Anglo-Saxon poems that can show us how the battles of Arthur's time were fought, and Latin writings from fourth- and fifth-century Gaul that give vivid glimpses of life in the Roman province that was Britain's closest neighbor and relation. I have not hesitated to use what is known about British life in earlier centuries as a means of imagining what is unknown about the world of Arthur.

* * * * *

I have given you one warning: I had better give you more. You are about to enter alien country. If you know a lot or even a little about the England and Scotland and Wales of today, it may hinder rather than help you; you are probably better off if you know nothing. At the time of Arthur, England does not exist; nor does Scotland or Wales: there is instead the island of Britain. I have tried to make things a bit easier by using modern place names most of the time, though I would rather have used the Latin and Celtic names that Arthur knew, as a way of seeing his land through his eyes. You may have already noticed one very important difference in my use of two familiar words: "British" and "Briton" in this book refer to the Celtic and Roman-Celtic people of the island and do *not* include the English, the Anglo-Saxon invaders. I think you will become accustomed to this rather quickly; I hope you will find Arthur's Britain, despite or even because of its different map and the strange names and customs of its people, a fascinating place to explore. And I think that once in a while you will find yourself looking into a mirror—Arthur's Britain is at moments surprisingly like our own world.

Before we can hope to know Arthur, we must explore his Britain. It is sometimes possible to see an age through the life of one of its important people: we can learn a great deal about nineteenth-century America by reading a life of Abraham Lincoln, as we can about Elizabethan England by reading a biography of its queen. We cannot do this with Arthur. Only when we grasp what his world was like can we begin to understand him and the part he played in that world; for the Arthur you will meet in this book may at first seem very much a stranger, not at all like the Arthur you know from children's stories or Tennyson or the film *Camelot*. Born in fifth-century Britain, he was what he was because Britain was a Celtic island ruled for centuries by the Romans. He led the Britons against the invading English, defeated them in a great battle, and won for his people a long age of peace. He lived in a difficult time, a time of great and often painful changes in British life. Some of these changes he probably found it hard to understand or to endure. Other changes he himself brought about or approved, changes that affected the course of Western civilization.

"More than the voice is the vision," writes a modern Arthurian poet, Charles Williams, "the kingdom than the king." I believe Arthur would have agreed that his kingdom was more important than himself and that the vision that inspired him and those who aided him was more important than any voice that could express it. So I shall begin by trying to show how Arthur's Britain came into existence and then proceed to Arthur himself. From there, I shall go on to trace the fate of that Britain after Arthur's death. Next, I shall examine the visions of the kingdom and the king given to us by the voices of poets, from the Middle Ages to our own times. In the last chapter, the Historian will confront the Poet: I shall explore the relationship between the poets' visions and Arthur's real achievements, which brought him his place in history.

2

The Making of the Kingdom

Imagine a young man born around A.D. 460 in the southwest of Britain. His family is prosperous. He grows up on his father's villa, a farm-estate of several thousand acres not too far from the towns of Gloucester and Cirencester. He can trace his ancestry back to a veteran of the Roman Army who settled near Gloucester around A.D. 100. He is, in the most important sense, a Roman Briton. Many of his forefathers married Celtic girls, some the daughters of local British lords; they served both in the Roman army and in the government of Britain. His family has been Christian for several generations. His father is a member of the senate of Cirencester and a delegate to the central Council of Britain. He himself speaks two languages—Celtic for everyday purposes, Latin for more formal occasions. He is well educated: he has been taught by scholars from southern Gaul, both at home and in the school at Cirencester, and his father has a small library. His way of life and much of the way he thinks are Roman, but Britain is his homeland. He is not very old before he learns that Britain is in danger, that it has not known peace for most of his father's lifetime, and that much of his own life is likely to be spent in battle or preparing for battle.

His present, like your present and mine, is what it is because of the past—not only of his own family but of thousands of persons acting and being acted upon through many centuries. How much does he know of that past as he grows up and begins to make decisions about his own future and the future of his land? Certainly he would learn of the events of his own century from his father, his uncles, and his grandfathers, and of the more distant past from his

9

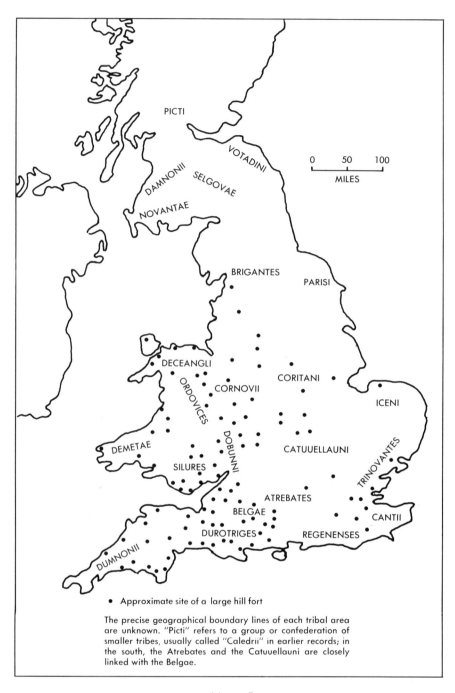

The precise geographical boundary lines of each tribal area
are unknown. "Picti" refers to a group or confederation of
smaller tribes, usually called "Caledrii" in earlier records; in
the south, the Atrebates and the Catuuellauni are closely
linked with the Belgae.

Map 1
CELTIC BRITAIN, ca. 100 B.C.

teachers and his books. There are a great many things that he knows far more about than we do, of course, but we have some advantages over him. Consider how much more we know about the American Revolution than the men who took part in it, and how much more clearly people of the twenty-first century will understand our own times. To live amid events is to be surrounded by trees: to live after those events is to look at a forest.

What our imaginary young man knew of the past, and what he did not know, shaped his present and his future. To understand that present and future, we must explore, more fully perhaps than he was able to do, what had happened to Britain in the preceding five hundred years.

*   *   *   *   *

If you have studied Latin, you share with this young man at least one thing, a schoolbook—Julius Caesar's account of his conquest of Gaul, *De Bello Gallico*. Boys are supposed to enjoy this more than girls, but I remember being thoroughly bored by it, though I suppose it did help me to learn Latin. Perhaps our young man was also bored, but I doubt it. These, after all, were his ancestors, and their kind of warfare, its weapons and armor and style of fighting, is to some extent part of his present and future training to be a soldier. One part of the book would have a special interest for him, Caesar's account of his campaigns in Britain in 55 and 54 B.C.

That first campaign had not been too successful. There was a difficult landing on the southeast coast (modern Kent) in which the Roman troops had to leap into the surf in full armor and wade ashore through a storm of British spears. Once the legions could form their battle line on the beach, shields locked together over their heads and short thrusting-swords at the ready, they moved forward as a single grim body that the British warriors, fighting from chariots and on foot, dented but could not break. The Britons retreated in disorder, but Caesar's cavalry transports had failed to arrive, and he could not pursue the fleeing chariots. "That was the one thing," he writes, "that cost us a decisive victory."

It did not help that when the ships bearing the cavalry showed up four days later, a number of them were destroyed by a storm. The Cantii decided to attack a legion foraging for grain, and the legion was close to defeat when Caesar himself brought several battalions to its aid and drove the British off. The weather grew worse; a British attack on the Roman camp was beaten off; and Caesar had had enough for one year. He would be back.

The second campaign went better, though it was hard fought. I think that young Roman Briton of the fifth century would be stirred by the deeds of his British as well as his Roman ancestors. In Cassivellaunus, the ruler of the Catuvellauni, whom the surrounding tribes had chosen as war lord, Caesar almost met his match. Cassivellaunus had one piece of luck, and Caesar must have cursed British weather, when a heavy storm damaged most of the Roman fleet. Ships had to be sent for from Gaul, and the surviving vessels repaired, while the legions were under constant attack. The British leader was clever: to meet the legions in a standing battle would be a disaster, but he could slice them up and wear them down by constant chariot raids on the infantry column as it marched northwest toward the Thames. Perhaps he could even cut the legions off from their shore camp and destroy them. So Cassivellaunus' men "dashed unexpectedly from the woods" to attack the guards as a legion dug in for the night; as the line of infantry moved into open ground, the British, in their chariots, "began driving all over the field, hurling javelins; and the terror inspired by the horses and the noise of the wheels" threw the Roman ranks into confusion.

What defeated Cassivellaunus, finally, was a characteristic of the British Celts that Caesar had noted among their kinsmen in Gaul. "Not only every tribe, district, and part of a district, but almost every family, is divided into rival groups." We can imagine that young Roman Briton nodding in sad agreement when he reads those words, much as a modern Welshman might nod at them. At the time when the Celts were the greatest power in Europe, around 300 B.C., when a man could travel from northern Britain all the way across Europe to Galatia in Asia Minor without leaving Celtic territory, they never formed an empire or even a nation—always they thought in terms of the family and the tribe as their political units. Caesar, as we have just seen, was well aware of this and had prepared to take advantage of it. The Trinovantes had no reason to be fond of Cassivellaunus, who had killed their king. Given Caesar's promise that they would not be attacked, they sur-

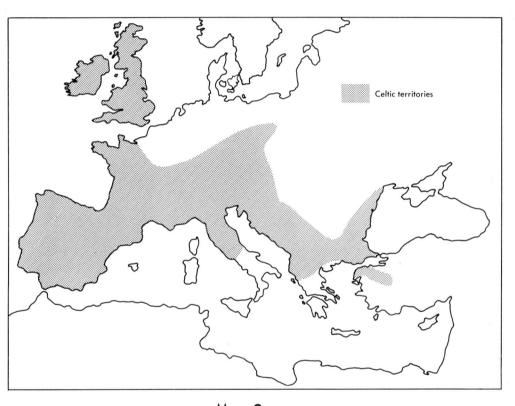

Celtic territories

Map 2
THE CELTS, ca. 300 B.C.

rendered to him and persuaded five other tribes (we do not know which) also to submit. Caesar, in addition to gaining a friendly base in Britain, learned from his new subjects the location of Cassivellaunus' tribal stronghold, a hill fort described by the Roman general as having "magnificent natural defenses, which had been strengthened by powerful fortifications."

Infantry and cavalry thrust, under Caesar's command, through the British troops defending the Thames and captured the fort—but not Cassivellaunus and his army: the British commander knew when to retreat. He also knew when to give up. After joining the Cantii for an attack on the Romans' coastal camp and losing a number of his men in a close battle, Cassivellaunus sent a delegation to discuss surrender. He may have judged shrewdly that Caesar was anxious to leave Britain, as long as he could leave with the appearance of a conqueror. Whatever the case, Caesar records, "I demanded hostages, set the annual tribute to be paid by Britain into the Roman treasury, and sternly ordered Cassivellaunus not to interfere with the Trinovantes." In September of 54 B.C., Caesar ordered his men to board the ships and left Britain for the second and last time.

Roman power had made itself felt in Britain, but it was hardly a conquest. Cassivellaunus, far from discouraged, went on to extend the power of the Catuvellauni over most of the neighboring tribes. Cunobelinus, his great-grandson, conquered the Trinovantes, built a great fortress at Colchester, and ruled most of southeastern Britain until his death in A.D. 43. From the Romans' viewpoint, Britain had been taught a lesson, and they might think about occupying it once they had made sure of Gaul. From the Britons' viewpoint, there had been a brief and rather unpleasant raid by the Romans, but British tribal life went on in its old way, except that it was pleasant and profitable for the southern tribes to develop trade with the continent, importing wine, excellent pottery, silver tableware, and jewelry and exporting grain, cattle, hides, hounds, and—depending on success in tribal warfare—slaves.

We know that there were discontented royal British exiles who asked Rome for help. We know too that Caligula planned an invasion in A.D. 40 but decided, or was persuaded, to call it off. The southern Britons must have been aware of the power just across the Channel. Refugees from Gaul brought with them stories of the might of Rome, and Rome believed that some British rulers encouraged revolt in Gaul. For almost a century after Caesar, however, no Roman army came to Britain. There were those in power in Rome who saw no profit in trying to capture the island; no doubt there were Britons unconcerned about a Roman attack.

In A.D. 43, troops numbering fifty thousand landed at Lympne, Dover, and Richborough. As of A.D. 47 the Romans controlled the lowland tribes of the south—the eastern and generally cooperative Cantii, Trinovantes, Iceni, and Regnenses, the aggressive confederation of the Catuvellauni, Atrebates, and Belgae, the hostile southwestern Durotriges and Dumnonii, and the friendly midland tribes of the Coritani, Dobunni, and Cornovii. The large group of tribes known as the Brigantes agreed, under their queen, Cartimandua, to a treaty of alliance. Roman engineers were planning a road system and Roman troops, using British laborers, were constructing the roads: this always had top priority in a new province. A city of Roman design was beginning to rise at Colchester. What had been, at the death of Cunobelinus, an island of Celtic tribes began in five years to become a Roman province.

* * * * *

Young men need heroes. That young fifth-century Briton could have found two men in particular to admire from these first years of Roman conquest. He could hear from Celtic bards and read in Tacitus' *Annals* the story of Caradawc (Caratacus), the British leader of the tribes that resisted the advance of Rome. He could learn from Tacitus' biography of Agricola about the commander who brought all but the northernmost portion of Britain under Roman rule and who encouraged the Britons to develop their society in the Roman style.

Caratacus was a son of Cunobelinus, and it was he who led an army of Belgic and Cantian warriors against the Roman invaders in A.D. 43. Defeated, not easily, in a two-day battle on the Medway River, he did not surrender, although most of his tribesmen did. Now a leader without a tribe, he would not give up. The Regnenses were no use to him: their king, Cogidubnus, was anything but a friend, and indeed showed himself (so it must have seemed to Caratacus) sickeningly eager to turn Roman, becoming a Roman citizen under the name of Tiberius Claudius Cogidubnus, and build-

ing a temple to Neptune and Minerva at Chichester. The Durotriges might resist Rome, but Caratacus had long been in conflict
with their rulers; the Dumnonii, even if they accepted him as their
war lord, could too easily be cut off on their western peninsula.
The choice was clear: he would go to the Silures, and fight on.

Tacitus writes that the Silures' "natural ferocity" was increased
"by their belief in the prowess of Caratacus, whose many unde-
feated battles—and even many victories—had made him pre-
eminent among British chieftains." It was Caratacus and the Silures
whose attacks on Roman troops and on the pro-Roman Dobunni
were responsible for the building of the legionary fortress at
Gloucester. The legion stationed there undoubtedly hampered
Caratacus' movements, and an attack on the fortress would be folly.
Caratacus, by A.D. 51, had gone north to the Ordovices, expecting
Roman pursuit and planning to meet the legions in battle on ground
of his own choosing.

We know from Tacitus that Caratacus selected his position carefully, but we do not know exactly where it was. Behind a river,
rocky ground sloped sharply up past overhanging cliffs to a hill
fort whose dirt ramparts were strengthened by stone. Caratacus
was heavily outnumbered by the Roman army that had tracked him
north, but his defenses seemed, even to the attacking general Ostorius, almost impossible to break. More important than the physical
defenses was the passion of Caratacus as he placed his men at the
key posts, shouting fiercely that "this day, this battle, would either
win back their freedom or enslave them forever." Tacitus tells us
that "every man swore by his tribal oath that no enemy weapons,
no wounds, would make them yield."

But Ostorius and the Romans, having after so many skirmishes
at last come to grips with Caratacus, were determined to make an
end of him. In several columns they rushed across the river and
charged up the rugged slopes towards the ramparts. A heavy fire
of sling-stones and spears drove them back. But the Romans had
dealt with hill forts before this, among the Durotriges in particular:
locking their shields over their heads, they moved up the hill and
systematically, despite the missile-fire, tore gaps in the stone rampart. Then "while light-armored auxiliary troops attacked with
javelins, the heavy regular infantry advanced in close formation.
The British, unprotected by breastplates or helmets, were thrown

into disorder." Caratacus and his men continued the now hopeless fight, slowly giving ground before the shields and stabbing swords of the Romans until they reached the very top of the hill. When Ostorius came to the summit, he found his troops surrounding a few prisoners, among them Caratacus' wife and daughter. But he did not find Caratacus. Not, surely, out of cowardice, but rather from determination to carry on the war though he had lost another battle, Rome's fiercest opponent had slipped away down the hillside.

He still had hope. Not all the Brigantes were happy about the peace treaty with Rome. Some of them, perhaps inspired by Caratacus' example or by actual messages from him, had attacked the Coritani until Ostorius forced them back into their own kingdom, where they had promptly begun a civil war until stopped by the busy Ostorius. Perhaps Caratacus thought that he could persuade Queen Cartimandua that with his help she could unite her subjects and successfully oppose Rome. If so, he was wrong. Cartimandua considered the allegiance to Rome her chief source of power, and she sent Caratacus to Ostorius in chains.

As he walked behind the legionaries in the triumphal procession given to Ostorius in Rome, Caratacus probably wished that he had died a warrior's death in his final battle. He was not, however, a broken man. He walked proudly, despite his chains, until he came before the Emperor Claudius. Then, according to Tacitus, he spoke with great courage and dignity: "If to my heritage and my rank I could have added only a modest share of success, I would be here in this city as a friend, not a prisoner—and you would not have scorned to form an alliance with a man of such noble birth, who ruled so many tribes. But as things are, my fate is humiliation, yours is glory. Once steeds and soldiers, weapons and wealth were mine —does it surprise you that I regret their loss? Because you wish to rule the world, is everybody else expected to welcome slavery?"

A mass of Romans stood watching and listening, "curious," writes Tacitus, "to see the man who had fought against their might for so long." Whether because it would please the crowd, or because he was really stirred by Caratacus' courage, Claudius pardoned the British leader and his family. He did not, of course, permit them to return home. We know only that Caratacus continued to live in Italy with his wife and children. To close his story, here is the comment he is supposed to have made as he strolled, a tourist under guard, through the streets of Rome: "Why should you, with so many and such splendid things, want to take our poor tents?"

Caratacus or Caradawc was an honored name among the Britons, especially among the Silures. The young man we have been imagining would know a fifth-century Silurian prince named Iddon whose grandfather, the first of a long line of rulers, bore the name Caradawc. He would also know a ruler of the Demetae named Aircol: the name is a Celtic version of Agricola, and a Briton, certainly a Roman Briton, could take great pride in this name too.

Tacitus was Agricola's son-in-law, and his biography portrays a thoroughly admirable man. It may give Agricola too much credit for certain achievements. Most modern historians see the book as presenting an exaggerated view of Agricola, but an exaggeration based on truth.

When Agricola was appointed Governor of Britain in A.D. 78, he had more knowledge of the island than any previous Roman commander. He began his military career in Britain on the staff of Suetonius Paulinus in A.D. 61. He returned to command a legion under Petillius Cerialis from A.D. 71 to 74. From both campaigns came the central experience of Britain, the ideas about what should be done, that shaped his decisions as governor.

Tacitus calls Suetonius Paulinus a "sound and thorough general," and declares that, as his aide, Agricola "got to know his province and be known by the army," gaining "fresh skill, fresh experience, and fresh ambition." The twenty-one-year-old Agricola's apprenticeship was not an easy one. Paulinus, with southern Britain apparently peaceful and the Silures and the Brigantes held in check, decided to deal with the Celtic priests, the Druids, who had constantly urged their people not to submit to Rome. That meant a campaign through the mountainous northwestern country of the Ordovices and the Deceangli to reach the island of Anglesey, which had become the center of Druidic religion. Drawing troops from the fort at Wroxeter, Paulinus established a base camp at Chester and then moved his column of troops on the dangerous path west. It must have been, even for the most experienced legionaries, a nerve-racking week of scouting along hillside trails, fighting off bands of British raiders, and cursing the mists that swirled down from the looming mountains on their left and forced them to march slowly or halt completely. Once they reached the coast, there were boats and rafts to be built under the watching eyes across the strait. Paulinus had no hope for a surprise attack—he must rely on a direct assault.

Thanks to Tacitus—or thanks to Agricola, who must have supplied his son-in-law with a first-hand account—we know what happened in vivid detail. As barges ferried the infantry across and the cavalry splashed through the shallows or swam, men beside their horses, through the deeper water,

> on the opposite shore stood the Britons, in a dense crowd and ready for battle. There were women rushing through the ranks of warriors, robed in black, hair streaming, hands waving torches, looking like frenzied raging Furies. The Druids stood in ranks, their hands raised to heaven, as they called upon their gods and chanted terrifying curses. The Romans had never seen anything like it: it filled them with awe and horror. They stood stunned, as if their legs and arms had gone numb, stuck where they were, giving the enemy a perfect target. The general urged them on, and this spread new life through the ranks—the men by jeering at each other worked themselves into a fierce desire to fight bravely. They thought it would be shameful to give way before a swarm of women and a group of fanatical priests: they advanced under their standards and charged to attack in a wild rage. The Britons died in the fires they themselves had ignited. The island was taken, and a garrison was assigned to keep it in submission. The sacred groves, which had been dedicated to superstition and to barbaric rituals, were hacked to the ground.

It was, quite simply, a massacre. We are tempted to see it primarily as religious persecution, but it was not. The Romans were tolerant of any religion that did not threaten their political power, as Druidism and, later, Christianity did. Tacitus puts the motive for the attack very plainly, saying that the Druids of Anglesey were inciting British resistance. He might have added that the region was a source of both grain and copper, a rich prize for the Empire. There are limits to how detached a historian ought to be: I find the wholesale slaughter of these Celtic priests, for centuries the most learned men of their race, appalling. I am not soothed by being told that Agricola and Tacitus were civilized men horrified by such Druid practices as human sacrifice. Civilized Romans left unwanted infants to die of weather and starvation on a convenient hillside. If I must choose, I prefer religious zeal to cold-blooded social and military practicality—which leads me to wonder what that fifth-century reader thought. As a Christian typical of his age, he probably saw God's hand punishing the heathens.

Paulinus was now in firm control, and no doubt he planned to move south and crush the Ordovices for good. Agricola was with him when a message came from the southeast: the Iceni had revolted; the Trinovantes had joined them; and the two tribes, led by Queen Boudicca, had taken and burned Colchester, slaughtering all the Romans they could find. The causes of the uprising can be called, probably too simply, economic; the Romans had taxed and exploited the southeastern tribes beyond endurance. Paulinus, 250 miles to the northwest, saw himself losing the whole province because he had disregarded or been unable to control the Roman tax-collectors. The lesson was not lost on Agricola.

If Paulinus had faults as a civil administrator, Agricola could admire his cool head and his boldness as they rode with the cavalry toward London through a no longer peaceful countryside. Boudicca's army had turned north and almost wiped out the legion that had been sent against it from Lincoln, pursuing the cavalry to the gates of the fortress. Paulinus had the luck that sometimes goes with daring: his cavalry reached London without trouble.

They stayed only a few days. Agricola was there when Paulinus learned that no help could be expected from the legion at Gloucester, whose chief officer was afraid to risk his men; he was there when the hard decision was taken that London must be abandoned as indefensible against Boudicca's troops, now heading south again. St. Albans, too, must be left to certain destruction—Paulinus did not have enough men to hold it. Both towns were looted and burned, their citizens slain by the thousands, as Boudicca's followers swept through them.

Paulinus, despite these terrible losses, knew what he was doing. His infantry had been ordered south from Anglesey, and he rode to meet them, knowing that Boudicca would follow. His reunited army was greatly outnumbered, but he could pick his own ground for the battle on which Roman possession of the province depended. "He chose," writes Tacitus, telling the story as he heard it from Agricola, "a spot in a narrow valley with a forest behind him.

He knew that the enemy could come only from in front, where the country was open with no hiding-places for ambush. Paulinus drew up his regular infantry in close formation, with the lightly armed auxiliary troops at their flanks and the cavalry on the wings. As for the British, bands of cavalry and infantry swarmed over a wide area. Their numbers were without precedent, and they had confidently brought their wives to watch them win, placing them in carts on the verge of the battlefield."

Agricola listened to Paulinus' calm practical speech to his out-numbered men. "Think of the fame that waits for you, so few, winning as much glory as an entire army! Make sure you keep your ranks closed. Throw your javelins, and then keep moving: knock them down with your shields, kill them with your swords. Do not think about plunder. Once you win, everything will be yours." The troops followed orders, the infantry holding the line and press-ing forward as the British charged and broke and charged again, the Roman cavalry driving in from each side, drawing back, and driving in once more. It was a long, hard fight until at last, near the end of the day, the Britons knew they were beaten. "They had trouble fleeing," writes Tacitus, "because the circle of their carts blocked the paths of escape. It was a glorious victory." And he adds tersely: "Boudicca poisoned herself."

Tacitus may be speaking for himself or echoing Agricola when he condemns Nero's decision to replace Paulinus with a new gov-ernor. It is clear, however, that Paulinus, who was devastating the lands of the Iceni to punish them, was not the man to restore the just and even merciful government that Britain needed.

If Agricola learned from that campaign, so would our fifth-century reader. Of mixed ancestry, he might applaud the revolt of Boudicca against injustice, for Tacitus typically arouses sym-pathy for the British, quoting them as saying: "We have our land, our wives, and our parents to fight for; all the Romans have is greed and self-indulgence." Probably he was more interested in the effectiveness of the Roman cavalry and in the contrast between the disciplined Roman troops and the brave but disorganized British.

I have been quoting from Tacitus' *Annals*, presuming that a well-educated fifth-century Roman Briton would own and read the book. He might, in fact, have both this work and Tacitus' *Histories* in their complete form. We do not, so we lack this superb historian's complete account of events in Britain while Cerialis and Frontinus were governors. We do have Tacitus' complimentary but brief remarks on both men in his life of Agricola. And we can learn from other sources something of the nature of Agricola's service under Cerialis.

For Cerialis, as for Agricola, his new post meant a return to Britain—Cerialis had commanded the legion at Lincoln that Boudicca's revolt had almost destroyed. In the ten years in between, Roman policy had concentrated on restoring and extending control of southern Britain. Towns were built or rebuilt, and the region generally became, for the Britons as well as the Romans, calm and prosperous. But the Brigantes' peaceful alliance collapsed in A.D. 68. Queen Cartimandua's husband, Venutius, had never shared her pro-Roman feelings, and when she divorced him and married his armor-bearer, he rallied the tribe against her. She was rescued by Roman troops, but Venutius now ruled the kingdom, posing a serious threat to the south. The situation called for a vigorous military governor; Cerialis was the right man for the job.

Tacitus sums up his achievement this way: "Petillius Cerialis immediately struck terror into their hearts by attacking the realm of the Brigantes, which is said to be the most largely populated in the entire province. After a series of battles, some with serious losses, Cerialis had been successful, even if he did not fully conquer, through the chief part of their region." And we are told that "Agricola's quality now had the chance to be seen, but in the beginning it was hard work and peril that Cerialis shared with him—the glory came later. Cerialis frequently would divide the armies between them to put his ability to the test, and when Agricola had proved himself, occasionally gave him the command of larger forces."

Details of the campaign are lacking. It is probable that Cerialis sent Agricola northwards with the legion from Chester through the western territory of the Brigantes, while he himself took charge of his former legion at Lincoln and marched to build a fortress at York. From there, he advanced through the eastern territory, forcing the Brigantes to fight a two-pronged assault. (Apparently the Parisii were cooperative—the Brigantes had not been very pleasant neighbors.) The major battle took place north of York, where Venutius had expanded and reinforced a large hill fort. It ended in a decisive Roman victory, though I suspect that this is where Cerialis' army suffered many of its casualties. The Brigantes, defeated in this as well as in other clashes large and small, were caught in a firm Roman grip when Agricola and Cerialis closed the ring by meeting to establish a northwestern base at Carlisle. Venutius had had northern allies, presumably among the Selgovae and the Novantae. Cerialis penetrated far enough into their territories to be sure that they would cause no further trouble for a while. When he left Britain in A.D. 74, his basic mission, to break the Brigantian power, had been accomplished, but there was still much that needed to be done before Britain could be considered truly a Roman province.

It was Agricola, returning as governor in A.D. 78 after a period of purely civil administration in Gaul, who set himself to complete the task. His immediate predecessor, Julius Frontinus, had literally laid some of the foundations: he had built the legionary fort at Caerleon-on-Usk, and from this base, we learn from Tacitus, "he conquered the powerful and belligerent tribe of the Silures, managing with difficulty to master not only courageous enemies but a treacherous terrain." Under the government of Frontinus, roads were laid to the fort at Carmarthen and further north, effectively enclosing the Silures within a chain of smaller forts. The Demetae, it appears, were pro-Roman and gave no trouble—they probably welcomed the arrival of a power that could protect them from the raiding Silures. Frontinus also campaigned against the Ordovices, using Wroxeter as a base, and had begun to build the legionary fortress at Chester before he was replaced by Agricola.

In his new role of governor, Agricola's third stay in Britain began anything but peacefully. The Ordovices "had almost destroyed a cavalry squadron garrisoned in their lands, and this first blow aroused the province. Those who wanted war rejoiced at this beginning, and delayed only to see how the new governor would react." They found out quickly enough—although it was late in the year for a campaign, Agricola assembled an army and thrust swiftly into the region where he had gained his first military experience. In a series of attacks over mountain pathways, "he sliced to ribbons almost the whole fighting force of the tribe." He had learned the use of boldness: with only lightly armed cavalry he forded the strait and surprised the British warriors on Anglesey,

who panicked and were easily forced to surrender. What Frontinus had achieved against the Silures, Agricola accomplished against
the Ordovices, and by much the same means—the legionary fortress
at Chester was completed and roads constructed to the new fort at
Caerharvon and farther south to finish a rough circle. This portion
of Britain, so long a problem to the Romans, was at last under
control.

Agricola had begun by making war, but he was at least equally
concerned with peace. It is this, I believe, that would have particularly impressed that fifth-century reader. He could read in
Tacitus that Agricola "knew how a province reacted and had
learned from other people's experience that weapons can accomplish very little if injustice comes in their wake." The new governor began by insisting on order in his own staff, and suppressing the
abuses of profiteering officials, giving the Britons "a reason to
cherish and think highly of peace." We shall take a closer look at
Agricola's civic policy after a brief glance at his campaigns.

Agricola's military role as governor was chiefly to make secure
the land he had helped Cerialis win in the north. He supervised the
construction of roads and fortresses as he moved north, beginning
in A.D. 78, through Brigantian territory. What had been Roman
outposts among potentially hostile tribes were now linked firmly
into a single provincial structure, so that "winter in these forts
brought no fears." This was not glamorous work; it was the pains-
taking job that had to be done for Britain to become more than a
constant battleground. Not that there were no battles—Tacitus
tells us, and again we can take it as information from Agricola himself, that "he did not allow the enemy any rest, but constantly sent
out raiding-parties. Then, having done enough to create fear, he
showed mercy and offered the attractions of peace. Because of this,
many tribes which before had clung to their independence stopped
being hostile and submitted to the control of garrisons and forts."

There were also some major military operations by Agricola. He
conquered the Selgovae, the Novantae, and the Damnonii; the Votadini seem to have been willing to accept Roman rule. With these
territories taken, and the usual forts and roads constructed, Agricola could very well consider that "a place for calling a halt had
been found inside Britain itself." The northernmost tribes, a loose
confederation called in the earlier accounts "Caledonii" and in the

later ones "Picti," were in appearance, social customs, and language different from the other Celtic tribes of the island, and the narrow neck of land between them and the rest of the island made a logical frontier. "This neck was now kept safe by garrisons, and the entire stretch of country southwards was securely in our hands. The enemy had been driven into what amounted to another island."

Tacitus sometimes avoids telling us everything he knows. My guess is that Agricola recommended drawing the frontier at this point, leaving to the Picts their "other island," and that he received imperial orders to complete the conquest of all Britain. I could be wrong—Agricola himself may have thought the conquest possible and recommended the attempt. Willingly or not, in A.D. 83 he began the chief campaign of his career, a combined land and sea attack on the Pictish tribes. By a northeastward thrust against strong resistance, he succeeded in establishing a firm base in the lowlands from which to attack the western mountains in the following year. He succeeded also in driving the Picts to unite under a leader named Calgacus.

In A.D. 84 Agricola led his troops against a large Pictish army at a place Tacitus calls Mons Graupius—the exact location is not known to us. As we have seen before, Tacitus can present the British side sympathetically, and he does so once more in the heroic figure of Calgacus. Roman historians took the liberty of inventing appropriate speeches for their characters, but whether Calgacus really said exactly these words to his troops hardly matters. Tacitus gives him the right words to express what he and others must have felt as they faced Agricola's legions: "You have answered the summons, every one of you, and every one of you is a free man. The last free men in Britain, we were protected until today by the remoteness and the isolation for which we are well known. Today, however, the limits of Britain can be seen: beyond us there is no other tribe, only rocks and waves. The Romans are unique: they are as eager to make war on the poor as to attack the rich. Robbery, slaughter, destruction—these liars call such things Empire. They create a desert, and they call that Peace!"

Tacitus pays tribute to the nobility of the British warriors and their courage and skill in the battle that followed. He notes that despite a strong attack by the Roman infantry and the success of Roman cavalry against British chariots, the Britons held their ground, and even began to move to surround the legion. I believe that fifth-century reader paid particular attention to what followed. "Agricola had anticipated a movement exactly like this, and he sent to block their way four cavalry squadrons, which he had kept in reserve for emergencies. In this way he shattered their lines and drove them in a retreat as desperate as their attack had been courageous. The strategy of the British now backfired on them. Our squadrons, following orders, galloped to strike the enemy from the rear. What could be seen afterwards through the open country-side was dreadful and grim. Arms, bodies, cut-off legs were strewn about, and the earth stank with blood." The eagerness of the Romans in victory almost caused a disaster—they pursued the Britons into the forest, but Agricola was able to restore order. By a careful encirclement of the woods, the British were hemmed in and flushed out, and "only night and fatigue put an end to the chase."

It had been quite a campaign. No other Roman general before or after marched as far north as Agricola. Most important, though the northern tribes were not conquered, the defeat kept them quiet through the next twenty-five years. But I do not believe that Agricola, when he sailed from Britain for the last time in the autumn of A.D. 84, thought of this victory as his greatest achievement as governor. Indeed, he seems to have resented the decision at Rome that prevented him from completing the conquest of Britain: he may well have regarded the battle of Mons Graupius as a splendid but worthless triumph. And proud as he was of his abilities as a soldier, he seems to have taken greater pride in developing Roman British civilization.

This is as good a moment as any to remind ourselves that "Roman" was a matter of one's allegiance and way of life, not of one's birthplace. The men who composed the Roman legions came from all parts of Europe, North Africa, and Asia Minor. Agricola himself was born and raised in Gaul, and he understood the nature of a Roman Celtic province better than most of Britain's earlier and later governors. Certainly he believed deeply in the basic policy of Rome, its practice of introducing conquered peoples to Roman ways.

Though earlier governors had begun the "Romanization" of Britain, and later governors would complete it, it was during Agricola's time that each tribe that accepted Roman rule was given regional self-government, modeled after the Roman senate. Each tribal senate sent representatives to an annual provincial council, the tasks of which were more ceremonial than political. With a few exceptions, the traditional central gathering-place of a tribe was converted into a capital town by Roman architects. A Briton remained a "citizen" of his tribe, however, rather than of the town —for example, while the capital of the Dobunni was Corinium, modern Cirencester, a member of the tribe, even if he lived in Corinium, was a citizen of the Dobunni. Agricola's motives and actions are made clear by Tacitus: "To persuade a people who until then had been disorganized, uncivilized, and therefore given to fighting, to become pleasantly accustomed to peace and leisure, Agricola gave private encouragement and official assistance to the building of temples, public squares, and private mansions." He did not begin or complete all of them, but the development of such towns as St. Albans, Silchester, Cirencester, Leicester, Exeter, and Caerwent was the direct product of Agricola's concern with civic improvement. Under Agricola, other urban communities also flourished: the *coloniae*, where veterans of the legions were settled after retirement, Gloucester, Colchester, and Lincoln; the fortress towns Chester, York, and Caerleon-on-Usk; the important commercial town London; the luxurious resort town Bath.

One look at the map (pp. 28–29) will show you how Agricola saw Britain. The southern roads existed before his term of office; the northern system of roads, and their relation to the south, is his creation. A Briton in A.D. 80 thought of himself as primarily a Dumnonian or a Silurian or a Cornovian; he knew that he belonged to a people he himself called "Priteni," but his loyalty was to his tribe. Tacitus, perhaps quoting Agricola, remarks that "nothing has been more useful to us in warring on their strongest tribes than their inability to cooperate. Very infrequently does it happen that two or three regions join to drive off what threatens them all; fighting separately, they are defeated together." Agricola thought in terms of *Britannia*, not, of course, as a kingdom but as a single province, and he made it possible for a Briton four hundred years later to think in terms of national as well as regional loyalties.

He also made it possible for that man to read, as I have been presuming he did, Tacitus' account of how these things came about. "He saw to it that the sons of the tribal rulers were educated in the

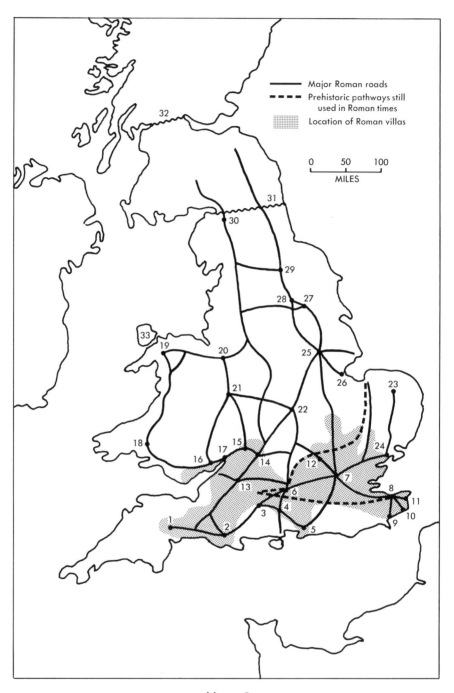

Map 3
ROMAN BRITAIN, ca. A.D. 150

1. Exeter, capital of the Dumnonii
2. Dorchester, capital of the Durotriges
3. Sarum, near modern Salisbury
4. Winchester, capital of the Belgae
5. Chichester, capital of the Regnenses
6. Silchester, capital of the Atrebates
7. London
8. Canterbury, capital of the Cantii
9. Lympne
10. Dover
11. Richborough
12. St. Albans, capital of the Catuuellauni
13. Bath
14. Corinium (Cirencester), capital of the Dobunni
15. Gloucester**
16. Caerleon-on-Usk*
17. Caerwent, capital of the Silures
18. Carwarthen
19. Caernarvon
20. Chester*
21. Wroxeter, capital of the Cornovii
22. Leicester, capital of the Coritani
23. Caistor St. Edmunds, capital of the Iceni
24. Colchester**
25. Lincoln**
26. Brough, capital of the Parisii
27. York**
28. Aldborough, capital of the Brigantes
29. Catterick
30. Carlisle
31. Hadrian's Wall
32. Antoine's Wall
33. Mona (the island of Anglesey)

*Legionary fortress towns.
**Coloniae—settlements of retired legionaires.

liberal arts, and said he preferred the natural quick-wittedness of the British to the trained talents of the Gauls. As a result, contempt for Latin was replaced by eagerness to master it. In the same way, our national costume became popular and togas could be seen everywhere."

We have been imagining a particular Roman Briton's reactions to reading Tacitus. How, I wonder, did he react to the stinging comment that author makes on some aspects of Agricola's policy? "And so the British were by degrees drawn to the luxuries that make vice so pleasant—arcades, baths, and lavish banquets. They called such new things 'civilization', when they were really the signs of slavery." I think he would have found in this passage, as in so many others, an explanation for much in his own troubled fifth century. Above all, though, I think he would have admired Agricola as an excellent general and a strict but wise and benevolent ruler, a man one could take as a model.

*   *   *   *   *

All of us know more about some periods in the history of our own and other countries than we do of other periods. Sometimes this is the result of personal interest; more often it comes from what is stressed in the classroom and in the books we read. I know more, for instance, about the American Revolution and the Civil War than I do of the period in between. Like it or not, war tends to excite our interest because it shows us the behavior of men and nations under obvious kinds of extreme pressure. Our teachers, like ourselves, find it easier to deal with dramatic conflicts than with the less intense and more complicated human activities of growth or decay in a particular society. What is true for us is true in other centuries. Gildas, writing in the middle of the sixth century, has only the most muddled notion of the development of Roman Britain, and while it is possible that a young man almost 100 years earlier would have clearer ideas, I rather doubt it. The Roman occupation of Britain lasted for some 350 years. What concern us in the centuries after Agricola are the things that affected that young man's life, even if he did not know about them, or knew of them only vaguely.

The northern tribes, for example, especially the Picts, the Selgovae, and the Brigantes, were never quiet for long under Roman rule. A series of uprisings led in A.D. 122 to the construction, under the direction of the emperor Hadrian, of a wall between Brigantian territory and the north. It is a superb technical achievement, 70 miles of stone wall with small forts at 1-mile intervals and sixteen larger forts, protected to the south by a great ditch 10 feet deep, 20 feet wide at the top and 8 at the bottom, with crossways leading to the forts and a rampart of earth on each side. Here, Hadrian said in earth and stone, is the northern boundary of the province. It is so impressive a work that one is disappointed to learn that it proved less effective than its builders had hoped.

The wall seems to have enraged the tribes north of it to such an extent that the Romans, on the orders of the emperor Antoninus Pius, moved their legions northward once more. In A.D. 143 a new northern defence was built across that "narrow neck" that Agricola had seen as the logical frontier. This wall was a huge barrier of turf rather than of stone, with a deep ditch to the north. Along its 37-mile length were nineteen medium-sized forts. Again a magnificent engineering feat, but in its results far more disappointing than Hadrian's Wall. Some forty years after its construction, the Antonine Wall was abandoned as the result of Pictish attacks from the north and Brigantian revolts to the south. Hadrian's Wall, neglected during those years, became once more the northern boundary.

Three times, in 197, 296, and 367, Hadrian's Wall was penetrated and partially destroyed, and each time it was refortified. After the fourth attack, in 383, the wall was abandoned. No fault can be attached to the builders. Had it been manned properly, it would have served its purpose, and indeed it did generally serve that purpose through most of the third and fourth centuries: the peaceful development of town and country life to the south would not have been possible without the existence of Hadrian's Wall. It failed to be a defense only when it lacked defenders, when manpower was drawn away from it to serve other purposes.

It has often been said that the remarkable thing about the Roman Empire was not its eventual collapse but its long endurance. The same might be said of Roman Britain. It became customary in the later centuries of the empire for legions in the various provinces to pick their particular general or governor as emperor. This usually led to a bloody struggle between different Roman armies until a victor emerged; and when he died or was assassinated, the whole process would begin again. Among the candidates for emperor through these centuries were a number of British governors and generals, and in each case Britain itself was affected by the results.

In 196 Clodius Albinus, then governor of Britain, claimed the imperial throne and led the greater part of the Roman troops stationed in Britain into Gaul, where he was defeated by Septimus Severus. As a result of these troop withdrawals, there was an uprising of Picts, Brigantes, and others, and northern Britain was not under effective Roman control for the next ten years. Severus succeeded in restoring order by a series of campaigns—he died at York in 211 while planning a new expedition against the northern tribes. His degree of success is evident: the northern frontier remained undisturbed through most of the third century.

Not that that century was entirely peaceful. It was during these years that Saxon ships began to raid the southeastern coast of Britain, while the Irish, called *Scoti* by the Romans, harassed the western coasts of the Dumnonii and the Demetae. One result of the raids, which grew in frequency and ferocity after 275, was the building of new walls and the strengthening of old ones to defend such towns as Colchester, London, St. Albans, Lincoln, Exeter, and Caerwent. The most important result was the appointment in 286 of Aurelius Mausaeus Carausius to command the *Classis Britannica*, the fleet that protected the coasts of Britain and Gaul. Carausius strengthened the fleet, set in motion the building of fortresses along the eastern, southern, and western coasts, and proclaimed himself emperor of Britain.

It was the first time that Britain had been thought of as a single independent country ruled by its own emperor. Most Roman Britons, it would seem, supported Carausius: certainly he had the all-important backing of the legions stationed on the island and of several legions in Gaul. For seven years he was such a good and successful ruler that Diocletian and Maximian, the coemperors of Rome, gave him official recognition as well as command of the northern shore of Gaul. His reign was brief, but it set an important precedent: whatever else in these times was unknown to a fifth-century Briton, I believe he would have been aware of Britain's first independent government.

It was a short-lived independence. Diocletian had only been

waiting for the right moment, and in 293 he dropped all pretenses and assigned Constantius Chlorus to recover Rome's temporarily lost province. Constantius defeated Carausius in Gaul; soon after, Carausius was murdered by his financial minister, Allectus. Allectus deserved no success, and had none—he withdrew troops from the north, but could do nothing against Constantius' legions, and London and southern Britain rejoiced in the triumph of Constantius. They might well do so: the northern tribes had seen their opportunity and swept south, leaving the weakly defended Wall of Hadrian in ruins. If Roman Britain had lost the independence it had enjoyed under Carausius, it might at least regain provincial stability under Constantius.

In the next ten years, Constantius justified their hopes. He drove back the northern tribes and refortified Hadrian's Wall; he continued the vital work of Carausius in constructing coastal defenses in the east and west. By Diocletian's orders, there was an extensive reform in the system of government throughout the Empire. Civil rule was separated from military, and placed in the hands of an official known as the *Vicarius Britanniae* (Vicar of Britain), based in London. Military command was under the *Dux Britanniarum* (Duke of Britain), whose headquarters were at York, and the *Comes Litoris Saxonici* (Count of the Saxon Shore), who was in charge of the southeastern coastal defenses along what had come to be called "the Saxon shore." Whether these reforms were completed by the time of Constantius' death at York in 306 is uncertain, but they were undoubtedly carried out during the reign of his son Constantinus.

Constantius had become emperor a year before his death, when Diocletian and Maximian voluntarily retired. It was natural for his son Constantinus to be proclaimed emperor by the troops at York. But only after seven years of battle on the Continent did Constantinus become unchallenged ruler of the western part of the Empire; not until 324 had he won the mastery of the Empire as a whole that caused later generations to call him Constantine the Great.

In general, the reign of Constantine, which lasted until his death in 337, was a period of prosperity in Britain. For one group of Britons, the Christians, it was most important for the Edict of Milan in 313, which granted them freedom of worship. There are no records of the development of British Christianity in these early centuries, but Christian writings from other parts of the Empire testify to the religion's strength in Britain. We know that three British bishops, from York, London, and probably Lincoln, attended the Council of Arles in 314. It is likely that in the new and favorable climate of opinion, a considerable number of Britons, especially those in the towns and villas, were Christians by the end of the fourth century. No doubt this spread of Christianity was strongly influenced by the vigor of the Church in Gaul after Hilary became leader of the Gaulish bishops in 360—there was constant communication between the Christians of Britain and of Gaul in the late fourth and early fifth centuries.

After almost fifty years free from serious disturbances, Roman Britain was troubled once more, in 342 and 343, by new Pictish attacks, and by the resumption of Irish and Saxon raids along the coasts. Constantine's son Constans, now emperor, visited Britain in person during these years. Accounts of his activities are lacking, but it is possible that on this occasion the office of Count of the Saxon Shore was fully established; certainly the shore defenses were strengthened. In the following years, struggles for power on the Continent severely affected Britain. Constans was murdered in 350, and Magnus Magnentius assumed power; three years later, Constantine II overthrew Magnentius, and took revenge on all who had supported him, including the Vicar of Britain, Martinus. Legions were withdrawn from the island to engage in these wars, and Picts, Irish, and Saxons, observing the weakened defenses, seized their opportunity.

From 360 on, the raids became more frequent, reaching a climax in 367 by a simultaneous and apparently planned assault. The Picts, joined by northern tribesmen who broke their treaties with the Romans, smashed through the thin guard at Hadrian's Wall and rushed south; the Irish in their curraghs, boats made of ox-hides on wicker frames, crossed their sea to land raiding-parties all along the west coast; the Saxons beached their long wooden ships, attacked or bypassed the coastal forts of the southeast, and roamed far inland. Both the Count of the Saxon Shore and the Duke of Britain were killed in the general collapse of the Roman defenses. If the invaders had planned to conquer and settle, this might have been the end of Roman Britain. They had come instead to plunder, and small bands of them moved at will through the rich countryside of southern Britain, seizing cattle, gold, and silver, and taking slaves. It was bad enough: about two years was needed for the Romans to regain effective rule of the island.

Britain's recovery from this massive assault must be credited to Theodosius, the Count sent by the emperor Valentinian. He was fortunate in facing no united enemy, only small groups of raiders that his own four regiments could easily subdue. He immediately set about restoring, and where necessary altering, the structure of British government. He appointed a new Duke of Britain and a new Count of the Saxon Shore, as well as a new Vicar with troops under his command as town garrisons; he set about rebuilding the coastal fortresses and constructing a series of signal and lookout towers far up the east coast; in the west, he rebuilt the fort at Caernarvon and restored or built new forts elsewhere; he supervised the strengthening of town walls throughout the province. His most pressing problem was in the north, and he solved this by a bold stroke—the Votadini in the east and the Damnonii in the west were given independence as treaty kingdoms, and so became buffers against the Picts.

Theodosius had much the same basic idea of Britain and the same thoroughness in carrying out his plans as Agricola centuries earlier. What Britons could still accomplish in the fourth century, and what they succeeded in doing to survive in the fifth, they owed largely to Theodosius.

It was not Theodosius, however, but a commander who had served under him in Britain, Magnus Maximus, who was remembered and transformed into a legendary hero by the Britons of later centuries. Maximus remained in Britain after Theodosius left; he achieved a high military position, possibly that of Duke of Britain. His popularity was probably deserved: he fought with success against new raids by the Picts and the Irish; he can probably be credited with strengthening the fort at Caernarvon and improving the roads to and from it; he may very well have married a British princess from this region. *Macsen Wledic* (Prince Maximus) is the name given to him in an eleventh-century Welsh story, where his wife is named Elen. In the story, she is responsible for the construction of the entire network of Roman roads! "Elen planned to build highways from one fort to another across the Island of Britain. And the roads were built. And because of that they are called the Roads of Elen." For centuries the Roman road north to Caernarvon was called by the Welsh *Sarn Elen* (Elen's Highway). Maximus evidently had the glamor that Theodosius lacked; he also had ambition.

Gratianus, who now ruled the Western Empire, had Theodosius beheaded in 376. It was an action certain to arouse the hostility of the western legions, and Gratianus' later behavior did not improve his relations with them. In 383 Maximus' troops proclaimed him emperor. Maximus, it is said, accepted the title reluctantly. I would be more willing to believe this if a capable emperor, Theodosius I, the son of the murdered Count, had not been ruling the Eastern Empire at that time.

Whatever his motives and whatever later Britons thought, Maximus took the one step that made certain the end of Roman Britain. He was no Carausius, content to rule the island independently. His goal was Rome itself. Constantine had achieved the imperial throne, starting from Britain: why not Maximus? We may allow him good intentions; Constantine's rise to power had helped, not hurt, the province, and Maximus may have hoped to be equally useful once he gained that power. But to gain it, he stripped Britain of most of its troops, taking as he sailed for the Continent many of the legionaries from the western part of the island. Gratianus' legions in Gaul joined Maximus, and Gratianus was killed by one of his own men. Maximus won control of the Western Empire, successfully invading Italy itself, but he was defeated and killed when he fought Theodosius I in 388.

The condition in which Maximus had left Britain soon became clear. The government did not collapse, the northern treaty-kingdoms provided a land barrier against the Picts, but both Picts and Irish, separately or in combination, were free to raid the coasts from the sea. The Irish, indeed, began to settle as well as raid all along the west coast. The few troops left in Caernarvon and Chester could not stop them from establishing themselves in Anglesey and plundering as far inland as Wroxeter; further south, they settled among the Demetae and looted Caerwent. The Saxons were not idle either—the eastern and southern coasts suffered frequent attacks. It was not until 396 that calls for help from Rome were answered.

Rome had been having problems of its own. Such Germanic

tribes as the Goths and the Vandals kept the legions busy in north-ern Europe and Gaul. Only after Stilicho, acting as commander-in-chief for the young emperor Honorius, had forced these tribes to accept peace terms could Britain be considered.

Stilicho was praised in 399 and 400 by the imperial court poet Claudian as the liberator of Britain from the threats of Saxons, Picts, and Irish. The seas are peaceful, he wrote, now that the Saxon has been conquered, and Britain fears neither the Pict nor the Irishman. Poets are not to be trusted as reporters, but Stilicho does seem—we do not know exactly how—to have put an end for a few years to the constant raiding. Any Britons who now hoped for a lasting peace, however, were swiftly disillusioned.

As Rome saw it, Britain was a far-off province, of some use, but of minor importance when Italy itself was in danger. Stilicho had brought some troops to the aid of Britain, but when in 401 Alaric led his Goths against Italy, Stilicho withdrew more troops than he had brought. How many men were left under the two military commanders, the Duke of Britain and the Count of the Saxon Shore, we do not know—certainly not enough. It was probably Stilicho, however, who created the new office of *Comes Britannia-rum*, Count of the Britons, and a new kind of defence force under his command. The new army consisted of six cavalry and three infantry units. It was small, but able to move swiftly throughout the island; it was clearly designed to use what manpower was available for the best kind of defense against raiders from the sea.

No one in Britain, particularly the legions that were left, was happy about the state of things after Stilicho's departure. What followed is almost comic. The legions first proclaimed Marcus, one of their own generals, emperor in 406, only to kill him a short time later when he proved unsatisfactory. They then, in November of the same year, gave the title to a native Briton, Gratian, a leader in the provincial council. Four months later, when Gaul had been invaded by Germanic tribes, most of the army wished to go to the aid of the legions there, while Gratian understandably thought that their most important task was to defend Britain itself. The army killed Gratian and looked for another emperor. They picked an ordinary but capable soldier who at least had the right kind of name, Constantine—and so, as Constantine III, he led them into Gaul. When he succeeded in relieving Gaul in 407 and winning

Spain in 408, it looked as if they had chosen well. In 409 the emperor Honorius gave Constantine official recognition, but Constantine wanted more power, and everything fell apart: his general in Spain, Gerontius, rebelled; the Germanic tribes resumed their plundering in Gaul; the Britons denounced Constantine and wrote to Honorius expressing their loyalty; Constantine was finally defeated by Honorius and executed in 411.

The upheavals of these years must have been terrifying for Roman Britons, especially when the Saxons, Picts, and Irish renewed their attacks. What matters most, however, is that in this crisis they found the courage and the ability to do something for themselves. The Provincial Council, which had existed for centuries as an honorary body without political power, took decisive action on behalf of Britain. It was the *civitates*, the tribal towns, who sent the message to Honorius, not the Vicar of Britain or any of the military commanders. This means, I believe, that the council, disgusted and desperate, rid itself by force of the officials appointed by Constantine. Their letter to Honorius shows that the Britons did not see themselves as declaring independence. Honorius' reply, however, forced independence upon them. It gave them the right and the obligation to train and arm troops in their own defense.

Honorius, hard-pressed by the Goths, could offer no help to Britain, but he probably meant to send imperial officials and legions as soon as he could. It never happened. If the British had any doubts that, like it or not, they were on their own, they must have been convinced when in that same year, 410, what no citizen of the Empire could imagine actually occurred. The city of Rome itself was captured and looted by Alaric's army of Goths.

For the men of the fifth century, the Fall of Rome had the kind of impact that the atom bomb had for us. Nothing would ever be the same.

*   *   *   *   *

Let us return to that young man we were imagining earlier. As I have said already, much of what we have just reviewed, the events leading to British independence, may have been unknown to him. But we have now reached the period when he could learn from his own father and grandfather what we can only guess about.

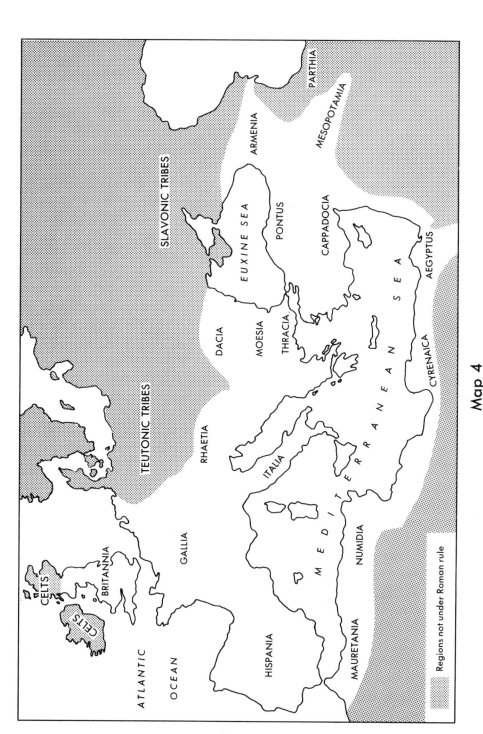

Map 4
THE ROMAN EMPIRE, ca. A.D. 150

CELTS

CELTS

BRITANNIA

ATLANTIC

OCEAN

GALLIA

HISPANIA

MAURETANIA

NUMIDIA

TEUTONIC TRIBES

RHAETIA

ITALIA

M E D I T E R R A N E A N   S E A

SLAVONIC TRIBES

DACIA

MOESIA

THRACIA

EUXINE SEA

PONTUS

CAPPADOCIA

ARMENIA

PARTHIA

MESOPOTAMIA

AEGYPTUS

CYRENAICA

Regions not under Roman rule

We can be certain not only that the Council of Britain acted boldly in 410 but that it continued to be active afterwards. But when we ask what tribes were represented on the council, how it worked as a government, how much of Britain was still ruled by it and for how long, we can find no certain answers. With the help of a few facts and a great many guesses, I shall tell you what I think happened in Britain during the fifty years before that young man was born.

Facts, for a start. Patrick (Patricius), known at least dimly to all of us as the man most responsible for bringing Christianity to the Irish, was a Briton. Toward the end of his life, he wrote a *Confessio*, a defense of his work as Bishop of Ireland that tells us something of his earlier years. It is too bad that places and dates were not his chief concern, so that modern scholars still argue about where and when he was born. If I cannot give you absolutely proven facts, I can give generally accepted probabilities, and these present a fascinating picture of Britain in the early fifth century. Patrick was born about 395: his father, Calpurnius, was a moderately wealthy landowner, and his grandfather was a priest (Christian clergymen could marry at that time, though the practice was being discouraged on the Continent). Patrick grew up on a villa-farm large enough to employ a number of men and women for work in the house and the fields; his father was a *decurio*, a member of the regional council of Caerwent. Patrick admits that he was a lazy student as a boy: "My faults stopped me from learning what I had previously read through." He is plainly uncomfortable about his failure to master Latin: "Now in my old age I seek for what I failed to gain in my youth." The point for us is that he could have learned Latin properly, that good schoolmasters were on hand. His education, such as it was, was interrupted in the most drastic way: Irish raiders attacked the whole region, and Patrick, aged sixteen, was taken prisoner. After six years as a slave in Ireland, he managed to escape and return to his home. That would be about the year 417, and it is most interesting that he found life going on much as before, and that his family urged him to follow in his father's steps by working for the regional government. He did not do so, of course. Convinced that God had called him to bring Christ's message to the Irish, Patrick entered the religious life, receiving his training in a British monastic community between 420 and 430. It is clear from the *Confessio* that it was the Church in Britain that gave him continued financial support for his Irish mission, and equally clear that some British bishops had their doubts about him later on. Was he really well-educated enough, they asked, to be the Bishop of Ireland?

What we learn in reading Patrick is that the civil government of Britain was still operating in the Roman pattern through at least the early part of the fifth century, and that the level of education, at least for the wealthier Britons, lay and religious, was of high quality throughout Patrick's lifetime (he died about 460). What we know of Gaul during this period gives added force to Patrick's testimony. The Gothic invasion of what had been the most learned province in the Empire caused many scholars, men who were fluent in Greek as well as Latin and who owned large personal libraries, to seek refuge elsewhere. For at least some of them, Britain, which had kept in close touch with Gaul, was the logical place to go.

I believe, then, that the Britons kept and used the system of education and government left to them by the Romans. Many of them surely still thought of themselves as Roman, and hoped for reunion with the Empire, while others enjoyed the freedom from imperial taxes and were happy to be on their own. The continued existence of the Council of Britain shows that for the men with the greatest wealth and power, the idea of *Britannia* as a single unit, a nation now rather than a province, was still strong. The actions taken through the period from 410 to 450 were decided upon by a group of men representing their particular regions but concerned with the country as a whole.

A few guesses, now. The office of Vicar of Britain probably continued, with the Vicar being chosen from among themselves by the Council. I doubt that the military commands of Duke of Britain and Count of the Saxon Shore were kept. The Empire in its richer days could support a large permanent army; Britain in its present state could not. Military defense was turned over to the regional councils, I believe: it would be the task of each *civitas* to train townsmen and countrymen as a militia that could defend its own area when needed. Remember that a considerable number of Britons had served in the legions, and that hunting was a necessary part of living in those days; it should not have been difficult, after

410, to establish the tradition of a locally armed and trained militia. But I also believe that the comparatively small permanent army of the Count of Britain was kept in existence for its obvious usefulness: its cavalry could move swiftly over the roads to aid the militia of any region under attack.

More than this was needed, however, to safeguard the island from sea-raiders. We have seen that during the final years of Roman rule, the northern tribes were given independence as treaty-kingdoms. What had worked for the north might work for the west. The Irish rulers of the Demetae were given official status by the Council; their kingdom, Dyfed, was assigned the task of warding off raids by the Picts and by their fellow Irishmen. A tombstone from this region has a three-line inscription that reads *"Memoria/ Voteporigis/ Protictoris"* (In Memory of Voteporix the Defender). Irish letters at the top of the stone translate the British name "Voteporix" into its Irish form "Votecorigas". The stone dates from about 550; shortly before that, Gildas attacked a ruler of the Demetae he called "Voteporius." The evidence points not only to a line of Irish kings, but to their official recognition by the British government: *protictor* was the title the Romans gave to the ruler of a treaty-kingdom.

Trust an Irishman to keep out an Irishman! That would be one way to describe the official policy in this case. But not all Irishmen could be given such a trust. For Anglesey and the mainland across from it, a different kind of treaty-kingdom was established. Cunedda, a prince of the northern kingdom of Gododdin, was persuaded to establish himself and his sons in this area and to drive out the Irish. The Irish were certainly not completely driven out, but Cunedda subdued them and founded the treaty-kingdoms of Gwynedd and Ceredigion.

It is my guess that these western kingdoms were founded by the Council of Britain shortly before or after 430. Irish raids along the coast suddenly end at about this time, and there must have been a reason. I do not mean to deny St. Patrick the credit he is usually given for ending the raids; I do think that the strength of the new kingdoms as well as reluctance to attack their fellow-Christians discouraged the Irish from sailing across to plunder that particular coast-line. There is, in addition, some evidence that an Irish prince married a British princess during this period—we can see this as either a result or another cause of the friendly relationship that developed between some eastern Irish and western British tribes.

The policy of treaty-kingdoms had worked in the north and in the west—why not in the east? Why not use Saxons to ward off Picts as well as fellow Saxons? Third time, alas, unlucky: the policy backfired on the Britons. But more of this in a minute.

The greatest danger to Britain was from within, serious as the attacks by outsiders were. The leaders of the Britons were men who combined Roman with Celtic traditions, and the Celtic habit was to think in terms of the tribe rather than the nation. I imagine that the Council of Britain was composed of men who varied greatly in their attitudes—some who, like Sidonius Apollinaris in fifth-century Gaul, would converse only in Latin and scorned "the barbarous Celtic dialect"; some who read Virgil and heard the tribal bard with equal pleasure; some who spoke only British at home and struggled with the Latin used at Council meetings. It was more than a matter of literary and linguistic taste: these were the men who hoped for a return to imperial Roman government, or who believed that British existence as a nation could be kept without the loss of tribal identity, or who thought their tribe was best served by cooperating with other tribes only for as long as it proved convenient. Think of the long American struggle to find a balance between the rights of the states and the rights of the federal government; it caused a civil war, and it is not over yet. Some of the Britons on the Council had learned the hard lesson we have seen in their history, that only by risking the loss of its identity as a tribe could any tribe hope to withstand a powerful and united enemy. Some of them, surely, had not learned it.

How long, I wonder, did the regional councils last? How soon did Celtic ways return under Roman names? I suspect that among the fourteen *civitates*—if there still were fourteen, and some had not already been taken over by their neighbors—a number had gone back to being Celtic kingdoms during the years between 410 and 430, and were represented on the Council of Britain by kings and princes who went on calling themselves senators and decurions. More guesses, now: by 430, I believe that the Silures had formed the kingdom of Gwent, using the town name Venta, and were ruled by a king named Caradawc; that the Dumnonii had established their own kingdom (modern Devon and Cornwall); and that the Cornovii were now subjects of the kingdom of Powys under a ruler known to us as Vortigern. All three of these tribes were less "Romanized" than the tribes to the east; town and villa life had not developed among them as it had among the Dobunni, for instance, or the Belgae. An eastern tribe might continue to hold meetings of its senate at which the elected members made decisions about regional problems and elected delegates to the Council of Britain. Not, I suspect, for very long, though such a tribe probably preserved the outward appearances and the Roman names. I think, briefly, that the Council of Britain became in fact a conference of tribal kings, and that the Vicar of Britain became, by their consent or his own power, High King.

Gildas refers to the head of the Council during the years after 425 as a *superbus tyrannus*. The Latin words mean "high king"; so does the British word "vortigern." Historians in later centuries seem to have mistaken the title for a proper name. What this suggests is that in his own time, perhaps against the wishes of some members of the Council, the *tigern* (king) of Powys who became *Vicarius Britanniae* adopted a Celtic rather than a Latin title.

He continued, however, to perform the functions of the Vicar. Gildas says that it was *omnes consiliarii cum superbo tyranno*, all the council members together with the high king, who invited Saxons to settle in Britain as defenders against the Picts. The policy is the same as that followed with the northern tribes, with the Irish in Dyfed, and with Cunedda in Gwynedd; it was standard Roman procedure, it had worked well for the Britons before, and the responsibility for it is clearly the Council's rather than Vortigern's alone. It may even have been under Vortigern's leadership that the western treaty-kingdoms were created; what he was remembered for was the invitation to the Saxons. He may have proposed it; certainly he was accused of it by later generations. A Briton born in 460, after the disasters that followed the coming of the Saxons, would have heard nothing good of Vortigern. If the policy that succeeded in the west had also succeeded in the east, Vortigern might have been remembered with honor. Or perhaps the Council would have been given the credit. As things turned out, Vortigern bore the blame for failure.

It was not failure at first. Your history books probably tell you that the Saxons came to Britain in A.D. 449—the books are wrong.

Recent historians have shown that the early sources for this date are inaccurate, as they are for other fifth-century dates, by about twenty years. The Saxons were settled, around the year 430, where they were most needed—near the mouths of rivers all along the southeast coast. They did what they were asked to do—they defeated the Picts. Sea-raiders themselves, they knew how to hold off an attack, and they probably retaliated by raiding the Picts' own lands in the northeast. For a dozen years, all went well.

Britain had done remarkably well on its own, if we make allowances for the occasional raids that disturbed one district or another. From shortly after 410 until about 442, the country had been at peace; it was remembered in later years as a period of unusual prosperity. That may not seem a long time, but in the histories of most nations such a thirty-year period is rare enough. In our own time only twenty years, marked by a severe economic crisis, passed between two world wars; only ten years separate the end of the Korean War from America's full involvement in Vietnam.

* * * * *

For years I thought that the Saxon "invasion" of Britain was a swift and large-scale conquest of the island by a single nation. It was not that way at all. For one thing, the "Saxons" were made up of varied tribes from the northern coast of what is now Germany and the western coast of what is now Denmark: there were Angles, Jutes, Frisians, and Saxons. The British usually thought of them as one people, and they seem to have intermingled and intermarried so much in the course of settlement that it is pointless for us to try to distinguish among them. *Saesneg* is still the Welsh word for an Englishman, and I shall continue, since we are looking at events from the British angle, to use "Saxon" as a short and convenient word for the invaders.

But they did not, as we have seen, come at first as invaders, but as settlers. They were given portions of British land in return for services rendered. The Romans, well-organized and set on conquest, had overcome southern Britain in just five years; the Saxons, in varied tribes and without a permanent army, took more than a century to occupy the same amount of territory.

The *Anglo-Saxon Chronicle* cannot always be relied on for accuracy, but one passage from it suggests how trouble started.

"They then fought against the Picts and had the victory wherever they came. They then sent to Angeln [on the west coast of modern Denmark], bidding them send more help, and had them informed of the cowardice of the British and of the excellence of the land. They then immediately sent hither a greater force to aid the others. Their leaders were two brothers, Hengest and Horsa." There is no reason to doubt the tradition that the Saxon rebellion began in the territory of the Cantii, and that Hengest was its leader. What happened, I think, was that the Saxons, growing in numbers, demanded more territory, and the British Council refused. The *Chronicle* records a battle in which "Hengest and Horsa fought against King Vortigern," and Horsa was killed—it does not claim a Saxon victory. But one year later, "Hengest and his son Aesc fought against the Britons in the place which is called Creacanford and slew there four thousand men, and the Britons left Kent and fled to London in great terror." It seems significant that Vortigern is not mentioned; it is more significant that this particular group of Saxons has spread westward from a small settlement on the coast to possession by force of one of the tribal kingdoms. How much can we believe of the stories told much later about Vortigern? Was his son Vortimer, acting perhaps as Count of Britain, slain fighting against Hengest's troops? Did Vortigern really cede a section of Kent to Hengest despite the protests of its king? And did he really marry Hengest's daughter, not out of lust as the stories declare, but to form a peaceful alliance?

What can be accepted is that there had always been some opposition to Vortigern on the Council, and that Vortigern, under pressure from British leaders as well as the Saxons, tried desperately to find some means of restoring peace. We can believe, too, that other Saxon leaders, inspired by Hengest's success, also rebelled. An alliance between the Picts and the Saxons is mentioned—this is likely enough. What we must believe is that the Saxons, after 442, seized British territory throughout the southeast. Gildas mentions a letter sent by what was surely the Council of Britain to the Roman commander-in-chief in 446: "To Aetius, three times consul, the groans of the Britons. The barbarians drive us to the sea, and the sea drives us to the barbarians; between these two kinds of death we are either massacred or drowned." There were still British leaders who looked to Rome for help—uselessly, since Aetius was facing the massive invasion of Attila's Huns. No help would come from Rome: Britain was more clearly than ever on its own, a separate kingdom rather than an imperial province. The *Chronicle* reports that "Hengest and Aesc fought against the Britons and captured countless spoils, and the Britons fled from the English as from fire." This suggests large-scale raids inland, after which the Saxons returned to their territories in the east; these probably took place between 453 and 457. Towns and villas were deserted. Many Britons sailed across the Channel to Brittany, where British colonies had been founded earlier in the century by western refugees from Irish raids.

We must rely on Gildas for what happened next. "The poor remnants of our nation," he writes, "to save themselves from complete destruction took arms under the command of Ambrosius Aurelianus, a modest man, who of all the Roman nation was the only one left by chance alive in the confusion of these troubled times. His parents, who for their merit were adorned with the purple, had been killed in these very struggles. . . . The surviving Britons regained their strength and challenged the conquerors to battle; by God's favor, the victory was theirs. After this, sometimes our countrymen, sometimes the enemy, were victorious."

We could use more definite information. Lacking it, we are compelled to guess once more. I believe that Ambrosius was a leader of the Dobunni, that his parents were descendants of the emperor Magnus Maximus, and that either he or his father was among the group of councillors who opposed Vortigern and sent the appeal to Rome. Later stories suggest that Ambrosius was much younger than Vortigern, and that he was responsible for Vortigern's defeat. Powys borders on the lands of the Dobunni, and there may well have been some hostility between the two regions. From Gildas' account, we can conclude that what remained of the Council of Britain appointed Ambrosius as Vicar. Gildas indicates that he was very much aware of his Roman heritage: it seems natural that he would believe in the Roman form of government and the titles that went with it. From about 460, Ambrosius was in fact ruler of Britain, fighting the Saxons with varying degrees of success for at least the next twenty years.

*   *   *   *   *

These were the years in which the young man I have asked you to imagine was growing up, and in which he would eventually serve in the British army under Ambrosius' command. I have been using all along the word "imaginary," but in fact not one but many young men really did have the same upbringing, were formed by the same history, and fought in the same battles.

You will not be surprised by now to learn that I believe one such young man was named Artorius, known to later generations by his Celtic name, Arthur.

3

Arthur of Britain

If you ask what proof I have that Arthur was really such a young man, I must truthfully answer, "very little." As far as I can see, what evidence we have points that way. Arthur is chiefly associated in the earliest sources with events in the southwest of Britain; he clearly continued the work of Ambrosius, and one tradition even makes him Ambrosius' nephew.

I base a good deal on his name. The likelihood is that he was given a Roman name by his Roman British family, and therefore that he had a traditional Roman upbringing, as much as was possible in those difficult times. Since the southwestern area appears to have been comparatively undisturbed before 480, the kind of upbringing I have suggested should have been possible; indeed, given a family determined to remain "Roman," it would have been a necessity.

It is true that during this period some Celtic rulers gave their sons Latin names or Latinized Celtic names. We know, however, that "Artorius" existed for centuries as a not especially famous Roman name, whereas there is no record of "Arthur" as a Celtic name until after Arthur's own time. "Artos" is the old British word for "bear"; the British bards, who were fond of puns, might have played with the name and the word in praising a warrior, but I cannot see the man's name as Celtic in origin. A comment on Arthur, made centuries later, says that his name means *ursus horribilis*, the savage bear. At a guess, this is the writer's false conclusion from the Welsh word for bear, "arth," and the Welsh adjective "aruthyr," meaning "savage". To be honest, it is *possible* that Arthur came from a Celtic tribe and was named or nicknamed

Artos or Aruthyr; it is far more likely, since "Arthur" is the form
of his name when he is first mentioned in a Celtic work, that he
was christened Artorius.

You may think I am fussing too much about this point, but it
matters. What I have suggested about how much Arthur knew of
the growth of Britain and its Roman heritage, what I shall suggest
in this chapter as probable about Arthur's own part in the events
of his time, depends largely on my belief that he was born and
reared on a Roman British villa in the southwest. Grant me the
likelihood of this, and a great deal follows.

As he grew up, Arthur would start by knowing the life of his
family's villa and of neighboring villas, of the Celtic settlements in
the region, and of the nearby town of Corinium. He would go on,
during his military service, to enlarge his knowledge by meeting
British lords who had returned to their tribes' ancient hill forts,
and by riding through eastern towns and villa-farms, some of them
abandoned or only partially occupied. Throughout his early years,
Arthur must have met a number of refugees from eastern Britain,
some of whom settled in the west, while others decided to take
their chances overseas in Brittany. Arthur would have encountered
a wide range of people and ways of living, from the still elegantly
Roman and generally Christian life of the villas to the clusters of
small stone or wooden huts that formed a Celtic and probably
pagan village, hardly changed by the centuries of Roman occupation.

It was, if I am right, villa life that was his earliest experience. We
tend to associate the word "villa" with wealth and comfort. We are
not entirely wrong, but a British "villa" could be as small as a
farmhouse with a few hundred acres of land or as large as an
elaborate group of buildings on a spread of 4,500 acres. What is
most important is that the villas were working farms; often in
buildings and acreage they had expanded through several centuries
from a family's small beginnings. If we think of present-day farms
and ranches and their variety in size and wealth, we shall not be
far off.

In the earlier centuries, there had been a brisk trade between the
villas and the near-by towns, and the owner of a villa often had a
town house as well. By Arthur's time, the villa was pretty much
self-sufficient. It grew its own grain; meat came from its own

cattle and sheep and from wild animals hunted in the neighboring woodlands; cloth was spun, woven, and dyed by the women of the household from home-grown wool, and hides were cured and tanned for leather; even pottery and metal tools could probably be made at the villa itself. The average villa had as its center a group of buildings that looked like a miniature village—stables, workshops, living quarters for the servants, and the owner's house, all built around a central courtyard. The whole area was surrounded by stone walls, less to keep enemies out than to keep animals in. The family's own living quarters, if they were even moderately well-off, would have been quite comfortable by modern standards: for one thing, there was central heating! Rooms were grouped on three sides of a main corridor. The two features of their villa in which a family might take special pride were the private baths, connecting rooms along one side of the house, and the large and beautifully decorated dining room, with its painted walls and ceiling and its mosaic floor.

If Arthur did indeed grow up on such a villa, he could not have enjoyed as fully as his fourth-century ancestors the pleasures of a country gentleman's life. The artists who had painted the walls and designed the mosaics were long since gone, but the beauty they had given to the rooms would still be there, somewhat faded. Homemade pottery did not have the quality of that imported in earlier centuries—though I do not see why families then, as now, should not have used on special occasions their best dishes and their silver service and glassware, carefully handed down from generation to generation, and more precious at a time when they could not be replaced.

I have already suggested the pattern of Arthur's education, the Roman system introduced all over the Empire. From the age of seven to twelve, he would study with a *litterator*, either a tutor hired as a private servant by the family or the master of a small school to which the families of the area sent their children. He would learn to read and to write (in Latin, of course), to do basic arithmetic, and to memorize and recite passages of verse and prose. From twelve to fifteen, he would attend school in a house located in the forum, the city center, of Corinium, and his teacher would be a *grammaticus:* he would study mostly literature, especially such works as Virgil's *Aeneid*, together with some history and philosophy. A small number of students went on, under the Roman system, to special training in composing and delivering speeches and the study of law as well as more advanced history and philosophy. In the earlier centuries, a Roman British boy who would as an adult be involved in legal cases and government work continued his education in this way after the age of fifteen, but I doubt that any young men in Arthur's time could be spared for this higher education. They were needed in the army.

Education never comes only from one's schoolteachers. Arthur, if he was at all an intelligent and curious boy, probably chattered in Celtic to the herdsmen of the villa and the small tenant farms and went with them as they drove their sheep to the hillside pastures. He might, of course, have been the kind of snobbish young aristocrat who wants nothing to do with the peasants, but I doubt it; if anything, I would guess that his family was somewhat worried about his becoming a "barbarian." He would enjoy the excitements of hunting, and have his own favorite hound—British hunting dogs were prized throughout Europe. He would learn what any good farmer's son must learn about crops and breeding animals; he would be taught to ride, and on his own horse, bought at a fair in Corinium or some other town, he would ride about the family estate and visit friends at other villas. His horse was far more than transportation. Ambrosius' army continued, I believe, to be primarily a cavalry force, and young Arthur would have been trained in the use of the lance and the *spatha*, the slashing-sword used for mounted warfare. All the young men of the villa itself and of the tenant farms would, in fact, be given at least militia training in building earthwork defenses and in infantry drill with spear, sword, and shield.

Corinium, modern Cirencester, where I have proposed that Arthur went to school, had once been second only to London in population, and had served as the center of government for the entire southwest of Britain during the later centuries of Roman rule. It was Corinium, I suggest, that became the meeting-place for the Council of Britain under Ambrosius while Arthur was still a boy. The town was no longer what it had once been (nothing in Britain was). How many of the industries and shops that had once flourished—wine stores, pottery shops, jewelers, bakers, butchers, blacksmiths, sculptors, cloth-dealers—were still there in Arthur's time? And were the public baths, that had once been a kind of gentlemen's club, still used at all? It was not the coming of the Saxons, or the earlier Irish and Pictish raids, that caused the decline of the towns. Urban living, so natural to the Romans, never really took hold among the Celts of Britain, and the constantly increasing burden of imperial taxation had caused the wealthier citizens to move permanently to villas in the fourth century. Corinium, like other Roman-built towns, continued to function as a market center for the surrounding countryside. Some shops probably were still prospering, such as the armorers', but fewer traders came to Britain from the Continent than earlier in the century. Corinium was a shabby remnant of what it had once been, but the town walls stood, the streets around the market square were still crowded on occasion, and the basilica was still used by the local officials.

If Ambrosius did make Corinium his center of government—and it does seem the logical place to me—the town gained new life as troops assembled and were quartered and messengers rode through the town gates. Corinium was better off than many towns: Caerwent was probably completely deserted by Arthur's time; Chester and Wroxeter served merely as trading posts; Silchester and Salisbury were mostly havens for refugees who scraped a living from the fields near town. Arthur, for good and bad, never knew urban life as we know it, or as his ancestors had known it. But I think he had some experience of the civilized pleasures of the dinner party, with its easy flow of varied talk—about hunting, literature, politics, horse-breeding, philosophy, art, commerce, religion. There may have been such distinguished guests as the Bishop of Corinium and even Ambrosius himself. All guesswork, of course, but southern Gaul was strongly defended by men who, between battles with the Goths, could exchange letters on Greek philosophy and give pleasant, refined banquets. We can suppose that men brought up in the same tradition in Britain would behave in somewhat the same way.

Sooner or later, though, the talk would turn to military matters —to the latest defeat or victory in the east, to new Saxon landings on the southern coast, to how long this part of the country could remain free from attack. Amid all the talk of his childhood, the talk of hunting and farming that varied with the seasons, and the usual neighborhood gossip, Arthur must have heard men's voices

returning again and again to the Saxons. The news brought westward may not always have been accurate, but he would know more
of Saxon movements in these years than we do. He was a child
when Hengest died and his son Aesc became ruler of Kent; he was
a schoolboy when Aelle and his followers, the "South Saxons,"
captured one of the shore forts "and killed all who were inside,
and there was not even a single Briton left alive." The Britons under Ambrosius were not giving ground easily, but as far as we
know—and this is what Arthur would hear as he came to manhood
—in most of the southeast the Saxon advance continued, and along
the northeast coast, too, they were moving inland.

I have assumed that Arthur was born about 460. As usual, there
is no proof; I have simply chosen the date that seems most likely.
Shortly after 475, I believe, he joined the British Army. Social
position counted for much among Romans and Celts, as it has in
most periods and countries: although it was possible to rise to high
command from the ranks, officers were usually appointed from the
aristocratic families. Given the background I have suggested, Arthur would probably have been placed in charge of a cavalry
squadron very early in his military career.

I have been deliberately vague up to now about Arthur's parents.
I have not had much choice: there is just no reliable information
at all. Much, much later stories refer to his father as Uther Pendragon, and call Uther Ambrosius' brother. I am very doubtful
about this. Something could be made of it; *pendragon* is Welsh for
commander-in-chief, and it is tempting to think that Arthur's father
might have been Ambrosius' military leader in the old Roman
pattern, that he was the Count of Britain. I have been trying all
along to suggest "probable" and "likely" situations for Arthur; I
must say that this one is just barely possible, but I think it unlikely.

I do think, however, that while Ambrosius may have sometimes
led troops, he acted primarily as Vicar of Britain. Vortigern appears
to have done so, and Ambrosius was more Roman in his ways than
his predecessor. So he would have appointed a Count of Britain as
head of the mobile field-army that aided the local militia. Who was
Count of Britain when Arthur started on his military career I will
not even guess, but, by about 485, I believe the Count of Britain
was Arthur.

*   *   *   *   *

We can only guess—again—at what Arthur was doing during the ten years or so before he became Britain's commander-in-chief. We know of very few specific battles at which he might have been present, but these were years of constant clashes between Britons and Saxons. Arthur must have shown his qualities as a warrior and a leader during these years, even though we do not know where, when, and how.

There are several peculiar entries in the *Anglo-Saxon Chronicle* that suggest one important event of this time, which Arthur would surely have known about and in which he may have been involved. The *Chronicle* notes that "Cerdic and his son Cynric landed at Cerdicsora with five ships," and that "six years after they had landed they conquered the kingdom of the West Saxons, and they were the first kings who conquered the land of the West Saxons from the Britons." At first sight, this looks simple enough: Alfred, the most famous of Anglo-Saxon kings, traced his descent back to Cerdic. But Cerdic and Cynric are not Saxon names: they are Celtic! And the dates given in the *Chronicle* contradict each other and are quite unreliable. Cerdic's conquest could have begun at any time from 475 to 495.

Behind all this, I suspect, lies a major event, the revolt of a tribal king against Ambrosius' rule. If Cerdic as king of the Belgae decided to assert his independence or to ally himself with Aelle of Sussex, Ambrosius and his military commander would have no choice but to attack. If the Britons lost the Belgic territory, the entire southwest would lie open to Saxon invasion. Cerdic, I think, was defeated and driven from his kingdom, but he returned with Saxon allies and succeeded in regaining a certain amount of territory, moving slowly northwestward from the coast. The *Chronicle* says that "they fought against the Britons on the same day" that they landed, and records several battles as they moved inland in the following years. In some of these battles, surely, Arthur would have been involved. Despite the *Chronicle's* emphasis on Cerdic's victories, it is evident that most of the Belgic kingdom remained under British control, including the town of Winchester. Cerdic was held in check, for the time being. He continued to be a threat, and would be one of Arthur's chief opponents during the major battles after 485.

If I have interpreted Cerdic's actions correctly, nothing could have pointed up more clearly the need for British rulers to remain united for their own defense. And if Arthur became a trusted member of Ambrosius' staff, he would have been involved as much in diplomacy as in combat. There would have been meetings with tribal leaders throughout the south and west, and missions to make certain of the loyalty of the northern kings. We can be fairly certain about where some of these meetings took place and about the names of some of the rulers, even though we can only guess that Arthur was present and influential during these consultations.

One place for such a meeting must have been Dinas Powys. This hilltop fortress was occupied in Arthur's lifetime, probably by Ynyr, king of Gwent. The king's hall, in startling contrast to even a run-down villa, was a wooden building, 40 by 15 feet, where visitors would join the ruler and his chief lords around a stone hearth. But the bowls on the table were imported from the Mediterranean, as was the wine the visitors drank and the olive oil used in cooking. Knives, swords, and tools were smelted and cast within the fort; bronze and gold, too, were worked into brooches, collars, and bracelets, probably by traveling craftsmen. Below the fort lay rich land for growing grain and grazing sheep and cattle and horses. Life at Dinas Powys was less elegant than it had been for Ynyr's ancestors in the now-deserted town of Caerwent, but it was far from crude and primitive. While the visitors ate and drank, they would have listened with politeness and perhaps with pleasure to the court bard chanting, in Celtic, of Ynyr's courage and generosity, and of the guests' triumphs over the Saxons. Then they would get down to business—how many men could Ynyr spare for that summer's campaign; where were the Saxons likely to strike next?

Arthur would find that while the British hill forts differed in size and strength, their pattern of life was much the same. At Degannwy, Ambrosius or his lords would consult with Cadwallon, king of Gwynedd; at Castle Dore, they would be feasted by Cynfawr, ruler of the Dumnonii, in his spacious hall. Arthur might well have traveled with messages from Ambrosius to the northern treaty-kingdoms, to Elmet, to Strathclyde, to Rheged with its royal fortress at modern Carlisle, to the court of the Gododdin at modern Edinburgh. Everywhere it would be the same: some of the Roman customs and tastes still lingered—in clothing, in tableware, in proper names (Ynyr is the Celtic version of Honorius), and especially in the techniques of warfare—but the basic way of life had gone back to being Celtic. How would this strike the aging Ambrosius or the young Arthur?

For Ambrosius in particular, I think it must have been a painful experience. Even Christianity, growing stronger among the common people as well as the nobility, was changing from the city-centered Roman pattern to the rural Celtic style of monastic communities and traveling missionary bishops. Acceptance of the changes was necessary; if the Roman British did not tolerate or even adopt Celtic ways, Britain could not survive. But Gildas, a generation later than Arthur, does not even try to conceal his contempt for the "barbarousness" of the Celts; his praise of Ambrosius as, in effect, the last of the true Romans suggests that Ambrosius would have taken no pleasure in what was happening. He may have had Celtic ancestors, but they were surely thoroughly Romanized ones; he lived to see the younger generation growing more and more "Celticized." For Arthur it may have been easier. I think he tried to achieve not merely a balance but a blending of Roman and Celtic ways. But there would surely have been moments of doubt and even agony.

There are modern parallels. Peter Abrahams, in his essay "The Blacks," shows us the African leader he had known as a student in London, Johnstone Kenyatta, "the most relaxed, sophisticated and 'westernized' of the lot of us," transformed into Jomo Kenyatta. "He had no friends. There was no one in the tribe who could give him the intellectual companionship that had become so important to him in his years in Europe. The things that were important to him—consequential conversation, the drink that represented a social activity rather than the intention to get drunk, the concept of individualism, the inviolability of privacy—all these were alien to the tribesmen in whose midst he lived. So Kenyatta, the western man, was driven in on himself and was forced to assert himself in tribal terms. Only thus would the tribesmen follow him and so give him his position of power and importance as a leader." Abrahams presents Kenyatta "brooding" and "bitter" at the price he paid to lead his people to freedom.

We need not presume that Arthur felt as Kenyatta did, but we should not ignore the possibility. It is likely that he began his life in a Roman villa, spent his later years in a Celtic hill fort, and died, the victim of tribal warfare, in a Celtic monastery. That he adapted is unquestionable; that he did so altogether willingly and happily is more doubtful. But I am looking too far ahead.

Not all of the hill forts housed lords and kings. Such forts had existed in most parts of the island since pre-Roman times, particularly among the Durotriges and the Belgae. Deserted through the long centuries of Roman occupation, a number of them were re-fortified in Arthur's time as temporary outposts rather than permanent living quarters. Cavalry units need bases for protection at night and between raids, and the small permanent British army was, I have suggested, made up of cavalry. The forts also served as temporary havens from Saxon raiders for British villagers. The Romans in their advance across Britain had the techniques, the time, and the supply lines to lay siege to the hill forts; the Saxons did not.

One more hill fort must be considered, before we turn to other matters. This is the one at Cadbury, where excavations are still going on. Here, some claim, was Arthur's Camelot. To be candid, I think that "Camelot" belongs to the Poet rather than the Historian. Camelot is never heard of in the earliest stories; it suddenly appears as the site of Arthur's court in twelfth-century French poetry. Where the name came from, no one knows. It is the fort itself that is fascinating. The top of the 500-foot hill had been occupied long before the Celts arrived in Britain; it was strongly fortified for use as a community shelter by, probably, the Durotriges, until it fell before a Roman assault in A.D. 45. The Romans forced the surviving occupants to settle in the plain below the hill, a policy they regularly followed after capturing such a fort. For several centuries, it remained unoccupied; then, from 250 to 400, the hilltop was the site for the worship of a Roman or Celtic god. What concerns us most is that around 480, Cadbury became a fortress once more, and one of considerable strength, size, and importance. A large rampart of stone, fronted by a walled wooden platform, rose above the earlier earthwork banks and ditches. Within the 18-acre enclosure stood a large wooden hall, suitable for a great Celtic leader, and foundations for a splendid church were laid, although the church itself was never completed. As at Dinas Powys and Degannwy, wine and oil imported from the Mediterranean was used:

some traders continued to sail to the west coast of Britain several times a year throughout this period. Leslie Adcock and Geoffrey Ashe have come to certain conclusions about the ruler of Cadbury: that nobody else in Britain at this time, Celt or Saxon, rebuilt an ancient hill fort on such a large scale, and that "it was the fortress of a great military leader, a man in a unique position, with special responsibilities and an unusual temper of mind." Adcock and Ashe consider that the unusual nature of Cadbury suggests that it was the site of Arthur's permanent dwelling.

I have ideas of my own about Cadbury. An army of cavalrymen would need a permanent base, well behind the lines of British-Saxon warfare, for several purposes: headquarters from which individual squadrons could be sent to several areas under simultaneous attack, and where the entire army could assemble before and after campaigns; training grounds for new recruits as well as veterans; breeding pastures for maintaining the supply of mounts. Cadbury was well placed for such purposes, because it was close to a Roman road that allowed both swift communications and rapid troop movements north, south, and east. The modern name "Cadbury" is a mixture of Celtic and Saxon words—"bury" is from Saxon *burh*, settlement; *cad* is a Celtic word that can mean either "battle" or "army". What the Celtic inhabitants called the fortress in Arthur's time there is no way of knowing, but *cad* must have formed part of the name. I do not see why the original name should not have meant something like "army headquarters."

Why such strong fortifications at Cadbury, which was not close to the British-Saxon frontier? We cannot be certain, but there is other evidence that the Britons were strengthening the defense of the southwest at this time. Two massive earthworks, now known as Wansdyke and Bokerley Dyke, were constructed. Both would require the combined efforts of many men, and they suggest that British defenses were under a single commander. Wansdyke stretches for sixty miles in an east-west line: a huge mound of earth with a deep ditch to the north, it is clearly designed as a defense against attacks that would move southwestward along two pre-Roman trails. It was built on the presumption that a Saxon assault would avoid the region of Corinium, which could probably take care of itself; the Saxons tended to stay clear of towns in general. Bokerley Dyke, further to the south, is a barrier across both a Roman road

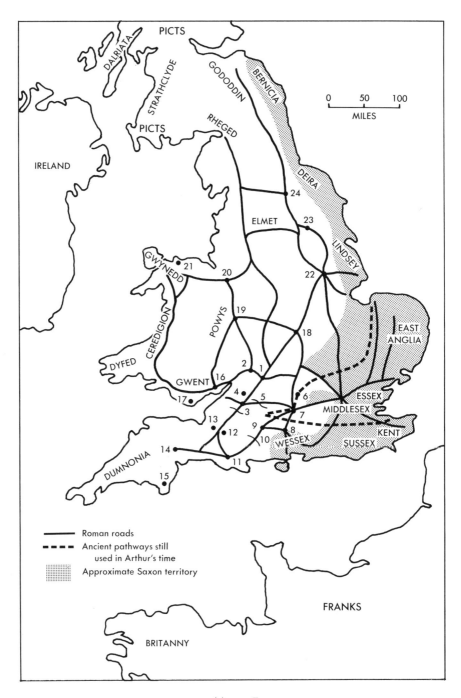

Map 5
ARTHUR'S BRITAIN, ca. A.D. 500

1. Corinium (Cirencester)	13. Glastonbury
2. Gloucester	14. Exeter
3. Bath	15. Castle Dore
4. Durham	16. Caerlean
5. Wansdyke	17. Dinas Powys
6. Mount Bodon? (Liddington Hill)	18. Leicester
7. Silchester	19. Wroxeter
8. Winchester	20. Chester
9. Sarum, near modern Salisbury	21. Degannwy
10. Bokerley Dyke	22. Lincoln
11. Dorchester	23. York
12. Codbury	24. Catterick

and an earlier but still-used trail: again the huge earth rampart is fronted by a deep ditch facing north and east.

It would help if we could be completely sure that Bokerley and Wansdyke, Cadbury, and the smaller hill forts further east were all being constructed and fortified at the same time. The best we can do is to note that the evidence is beginning to point towards such a conclusion. That so much defensive fortification went on in roughly the same period suggests to me a deliberate, centrally controlled policy, and it suggests also that the Britons were expecting a large-scale Saxon assault. Just such an assault came, in fact, at some time between 490 and 500.

I have been dwelling on British defense measures, the cementing of alliances with tribal rulers, the construction of forts and ramparts. This is the unglamorous side of warfare, much less exciting than the clash of armies but no less important. I believe that this defense policy was carefully planned and carried out between 480 and 490. It may have been conceived by Ambrosius, or by Arthur himself. Certainly Arthur would have had a major role in such a task after 485.

*   *   *   *   *

Dates are a problem, as usual. All I can do is once more suggest what I think makes the most sense: that Ambrosius was born about 435, became ruler of Britain about 460, and died about 495; that Arthur became Count of Britain about 485 and fought his major campaigns during the following ten years.

There is no doubt at all among historians that the British won a decisive victory over the Saxons during these years. Gildas states specifically that "in the year of the siege of Mons Badonicus" there was "almost the last but not the least slaughter of our cruel enemies." Gildas seems—his prose is sometimes not very clear—to add that the siege of Mount Badon took place in the year of his own birth, forty-four years before he wrote his book. This would place the battle at some time between 495 and 500.

Gildas does not mention Arthur at all in his book. If he were to mention him anywhere, we would expect it to be in connection with this battle. All kinds of suggestions have been made about Gildas' reasons for ignoring Arthur, including a personal grudge. I see no reason for going into these. What is significant is that Gildas does not name any British leader in connection with Mount Badon, not even Ambrosius whom he so much admired. A major victory does not just happen—it requires a general. And all later writers agree that the general was Arthur.

Mount Badon was the decisive battle, but it came as the climax of a series of battles. Nennius, writing three hundred years later, is not the most trustworthy guide, but he is all we have. Here, then, is Nennius' account of Arthur's campaigns:

> Arthur fought against the Saxons in those days accompanied by the kings of the Britons, but he himself was the commander in the battles. The first battle was at the mouth of the river Glein. The second, third, fourth, and fifth were on the banks of another river, called Dubglas, in the region of Linnuis. The sixth battle was on the river called Bassas. The seventh was in the wood of Celidon, that is, Cat Coit Celidon. The eighth was by Castle Guinnion, in which Arthur carried the image of the Blessed Virgin Mary on his shoulders, and the pagans were routed with great slaughter that day, by the power of Our Lord Jesus Christ and the Virgin Mary His Mother. The ninth battle was in the City of the Legion. The tenth was fought on the bank of the river called Tribruit. The eleventh was on the hill called Agned. The twelfth battle was at Mount Badon, in which on a single day 960 men fell in one onslaught of Arthur's and no one overcame them but himself alone, and in all of the battles he was the victor.

We can add to Nennius the brief entry in the *Annales Cambriae:* "The Battle of Badon, in which Arthur carried the Cross of our Lord Jesus Christ on his shoulders for three days and three nights, and the Britons were victorious." This chronicle was written about 150 years later than Nennius', but it differs, as you can see, on certain details and seems to be based on other sources of information than Nennius.

To what extent can we believe Nennius? Several things encourage at least a degree of belief. Nennius does not claim royal birth for Arthur; he refers to him simply as *miles,* a soldier, and states that "many men were more nobly born than he was." This can be taken to mean just what it says. It does not imply that Arthur was not wellborn; it does indicate that his father was not among the greatest lords in Britain. (That is one reason why I rejected earlier the story that makes Ambrosius Arthur's uncle.) In Roman times, men of quite low birth could rise very high: the Emperor Vespasian came from a very poor, lower-class family and achieved high military rank and eventually the imperial throne because of his outstanding abilities as a soldier. The picture I have so far presented of Arthur will hold together—a man born into a moderately wealthy family and earning the post of commander-in-chief by his military and diplomatic service to Ambrosius.

Arthur's military and political position is fairly clear in Nennius. He is not one of the British rulers; he fights—surely with troops of his own rather than by himself!—*cum regibus Brittonum*, together with, as an ally of, the British kings. Nevertheless he outranks them: *sed ipse erat dux bellorum*, but it is he who was the commander-in-chief, the war lord, the *pendragon*. *Dux bellorum* is not an official title, but *dux* indicated high rank in later Roman times. A *dux bellorum* with his own army, acting in alliance with and as war lord of the British kings, is clearly in the tradition of the Count of Britain with his mobile field army.

Some writers have suggested that the office and command of the Count of Britain were revived by or for Arthur. My own view has, I hope, been clear: I do not see why we should presume that the office needed to be revived. Why should it not have continued throughout the fifth century with exactly the function that is indicated by Nennius, as a small permanent cavalry force that could aid the local rulers?

The Arthur presented by Nennius can therefore be believed in as a man with a traditional military rank. What about the battles? Did they really take place? Most of them can be accepted as true, for what may seem a rather odd reason—with two exceptions, we cannot identify the place names with any certainty! Nennius probably could not have identified them either. If he had been making things up, he would have been far more likely to use well-known places as the sites of the battles; it sounds instead as if he is simply passing on information from earlier authors.

The historian of Arthur at this point is inclined to envy the historian of General Grant. Grant's battles can be reconstructed very precisely, location, landscape, troop movements, and all. We cannot do this with Arthur. Instead, I shall suggest possible places and the nature of the fighting. I am inclined to be suspicious of

Nennius' arithmetic—twelve is such a neat number for the total of battles—and of his sequence. There may have been fewer than twelve major conflicts; they may have been in a different order; and I doubt that Arthur won all of them. But there is no reason to doubt that Mount Badon was the final battle and that Arthur won a great and lasting victory there.

We can picture, dimly, the army that Arthur led. It was probably not large, three hundred men at the most. The warriors would be recruited from the more adventurous young men among the tribes throughout the kingdom, and from the neighboring British treaty-kingdoms. Attempts have been made to present Arthur's cavalry as heavily armored, but I simply cannot believe this. Cavalry had become the most important part of the later Roman army, but when the Romans tried to use heavy armor for the cavalry, it did not work out very well. The whole pattern of warfare was changed by the introduction of the metal stirrup, which enabled a heavily armored man to brace himself as he charged. There have been quite clever attempts to suggest that Arthur's cavalry could have had metal stirrups, but in fact such stirrups were not used in western Europe until the early eighth century. We had better be content to picture Arthur's warriors as not very different from earlier Roman cavalrymen, wearing helmets that were basically iron-framed leather caps with attached neck and cheek guards, coats made of intertwined metal rings worn over leather tunics, leather breeches, and leather boots. Their round shields were either of iron or iron-plated wood; their weapons were 6-foot lances with wooden shafts and four-sided iron heads, and long swords designed for slashing rather than stabbing. Their horses would be given some protection by leather or metal-and-leather trappings; stirrups of leather or of rope would be used to enable the men to mount and to stay on the horses. We can add some touches of color, Roman and Celtic: one man would carry a pennon with the symbol of the red dragon, the traditional flag of the imperial cavalry; many of the warriors would wear golden neck-chains and arm-bracelets, and fasten their cloaks with golden brooches.

Against the Saxons, who were exclusively foot-soldiers, the British cavalry as we have just pictured them could be extremely effective. Only about twenty years before Arthur's major campaigns, Sidonius Apollinaris in southern Gaul wrote to his brother-in-law

Ecdicius from the city of Clermont, surrounded by Gothic invaders but still defending itself strongly: "Whatever we have to
look forward to—whether hope or despair—still we are determined
to have you with us as our leader." Four years later Sidonius praised
Ecdicius' heroic charge through the Gothic infantry: "At noon
and clear through the open countryside you came with a mere
troop of eighteen cavalry through some thousands of Goths."
Ecdicius' reception by the townspeople is vividly pictured: "Some
kissed away the dust from you, some seized the bridles smeared
with foam and blood, some turned over the saddles drenched in
sweat, others unbuckled the clasps to detach the cheek-pieces of
your helmet so that you could take it off."

What could happen in southern Gaul could happen in Britain.
A highly disciplined cavalry force, skillfully used in combination
with local infantry and mounted warriors—this is how we must see
Arthur's troops as they fought the Saxon foot soldiers. Nennius'
list indicates that most of the battles took place at river fords. This
is in keeping with both Celtic and Saxon customs and makes us
even more inclined to trust Nennius' list of Arthur's battles.

All attempts to suggest possible locales for these battles result in
a pattern so clear that we can call it a fact. The battles took place
in widely separated parts of Britain, not only in the southwest.

The first battle in Nennius' list has been placed by various historians in three different regions. One is as likely as another, but I
am inclined to think it was in the northeast, as were the next four,
since "Linnuis" is probably the Saxon kingdom of Lindsey. Taken
together, the five battles suggest that Arthur's men rode from their
base at Cadbury along the roughly diagonal line of the Roman
roads to the region east of Lincoln, where in one campaign or
several they forced the Saxons back towards their coastal territories.

No one knows where the river Bassas is or was; the southeast is
as good a guess as any. For the seventh battle, Nennius is very
explicit: "Cat Coit Celidon" means, in Celtic, "The Battle of the
Caledonian Wood," and this can only refer to the northern region
west of Gododdin. What was Arthur doing up there, presuming
that Nennius is accurate? The enemy in this case must have been
the Picts, joined possibly by those Irish warriors who had founded
the kingdom of Dalriata and who eventually gave their Latin name,
Scoti, to the northern kingdom of Scotland. Since the Saxons and

the Picts sometimes formed alliances, they might have done so for the battles in Lindsey, and the Saxons may have persuaded the Picts and the Scots to attack the northern treaty-kingdoms as a way of keeping the British busy on several fronts at the same time. If Nennius' list is not in correct sequence, or if Bassas was actually a river in the northeast, it is easy to imagine Arthur, after his successes in Lindsey, answering a call for help from the northern rulers.

Castle Guinnion could, just possibly, be Nennius' version of Winchester, but Caerwent has also been suggested. If it was Winchester, Arthur is back in the south, fighting against Cerdic's West Saxons; if it was Caerwent, then Arthur might have been fighting Pictish raiders on the coast of Gwent. The City of the Legion, which probably means Caerleon-on-Usk, suggests at least one such battle in this area. Tribruit is usually placed in the same general region as the Caledonian Wood: either Arthur moved north once more against the Picts and Scots, or else this battle took place during the same northern campaign and Nennius has placed it out of sequence. No one has been able to suggest a reasonable location for "the hill called Agned"; we might as well guess that it was one of the southern hill forts and let it go at that. Badon is generally accepted as in the south, and the battle was certainly against an unusually large Saxon army.

How much time all this took, how often Arthur may have returned to headquarters at Cadbury or conferred with the Council of Britain at Corinium, we cannot say. Certainly it must have taken five years, probably more.

However doubtful we may be about accepting Nennius' list in its entirety, the picture it gives of Arthur with his cavalry aiding various tribal leaders throughout Britain agrees with what we know of Saxon pressures along the east coast and in the south at this time. The further suggestion of Pictish raiding on the west coast and attacks on the northern treaty-kingdoms fits into the earlier history of Britain: the Picts had always been ready to take advantage of any disruption in the south. And Arthur's activities show him continuing, as we might expect, in the military tradition inherited from the Romans.

Though we cannot give any details of these particular battles and the men who fought them, we have some notion of what they were like, thanks to both British and Saxon poets. Their poems come from a later time than Arthur's, but the types of men, the weapons, the techniques of combat had not changed much since Arthur's day. Surely a bard at Cadbury would have seen the same kind of young warrior that Aneirin saw and praised one hundred years later in the north:

> Man's mettle, youth's years,
> Courage for combat:
> Swift thick-maned stallions
> Beneath a fine stripling's thighs,
> Broad lightweight buckler
> On a slim steed's crupper,
> Glittering blue blades,
> Gold-bordered garments.

And for such a young man, the same lament would be raised after a battle:

> The blood-soaked field
> Before the marriage-feast,
> Foodstuff for crows
> Before the burial.
> A dear comrade, Owain;
> Vile, his cover of crows.

Surely, too, there were brawny veterans who "guzzled mead-suppers at midnight," who "drove the foe out of house and home-land" and "slew Saxons at least once a week." Aneirin gives us terse, grim pictures of cavalrymen in action, and we can imagine Arthur's troops in these lines:

> He has slaughtered with shaft and with blade
> And with savage hooves men in battle.
>   .   .   .   .
>
> Superb courage, strife-embroiled rider,
> Red reaper, he hungered for battle.
> Fervent fighter, wherever he heard
> The clash with that country's horde he charged,

THE PIERPONT MORGAN LIBRARY

Shield upon shield. He would lift a spear
Like a glass of sparkling wine.

.   .   .   .   .   .

He planted ashen shafts with squared
Hand, atop a steaming stallion.
He slashed with a sharp bloodstained blade.
As reapers reap when weather turns,
So Marchlew made the blood gush out.

.   .   .   .

When Cadwal charged in the green of dawn
A cry went up wherever he came.
He would leave shields shattered, in splinters.

.   .   .   .

Rent the front of his shield, when he heard
The war-cry, he spared none he pursued.
He'd not turn from a battle till blood
Flowed, like rushes hewed men who'd not flee.

If we want to picture Arthur's men as they galloped along the Roman roads, we can do so once more through Aneirin:

> Speedy steeds and dark armour and shields,
> Spear-shafts held high and spear-points sharp-edged,
> And glittering coats-of-mail and swords.

On the Saxon side, the poet who composed *Beowulf* lets us see and hear the foot soldiers marching along a Roman road to a king's great hall:

> The road was paved; it showed those warriors
> the way. Their corslets were gleaming,
> the strong links of shining chain-mail
> clinked together. . . .
> Then they sat on a bench; the brave men's
> armour sang. The seafarers' gear
> stood all together, a grey-tipped forest
> of ash-spears.

And we can see the Saxon shield-ring formed, as Arthur and his men would often have seen it, in *The Battle of Maldon*:

> Byrhtnoth and his warriors awaited them,
> Ready for battle: he ordered his men
> To form a phalanx with their shields, and to stand firm
> Against the onslaught of the enemy. . . .
> They hurled their spears, hard as files,
> And sent sharp darts flying from their hands.
> Bow strings were busy, shield parried point,
> Bitter was the battle. Brave men fell
> On both sides, youths choking in the dust.

The kind of warfare Arthur fought is shown in two poems by Taliesin, in which one battle takes place at a river crossing, the other in the field below a fortified hillside:

> Like waves roaring harsh onto shore
> I saw savage men in war-bands:
> And after morning's fray, torn flesh.

Defending Gwen Ystrad one saw
A thin rampart and lone weary men.
At the ford I saw men stained with blood
Downing arms before a grey-haired lord:
They wished peace, for they found the way barred,
Hands crossed, on the strand, cheeks pallid.

.   .   .   .

Shouted Fflamddwyn, big at boasting,
"Have the hostages come? Are they ready?"
Answered Owain, bane of the East,
"They've not come, are not here, are not ready.
And a cub of Coel's line must be pressed
Hard before he'd render one hostage."
Shouted Urien, lord of Yrechwydd,
"If a meeting for concord's to come,
Let our banners rise on the mountain
And let our faces lift over the rim
And let our spears rise over men's heads
And let us charge Fflamddwyn amid his men
And let us kill both him and his comrades."
   Before Argoed Llwyfain
      There was many a dead man.
      Crows were crimsoned from warriors.
And the tribe charged with its chieftain.

The battle for which we would most like some details is, of course, the climactic one at Mount Badon. Arthur's other battles were probably small compared with this. Everything indicates that the Saxon kings of the southeast had formed an alliance—Cerdic of Wessex, Aesc of Kent, and Aelle of Sussex, with Aelle as their commander-in-chief. Aelle is the only one of these early kings to be called *Bretwalda*, a title of special significance meaning "ruler of Britain." We know almost nothing about Aelle's conquests, but to earn such a title he must have been a noteworthy leader. Gildas refers to the battle as a siege; all the sources indicate that Badon was a hill or mountain; one source tells us that the fighting lasted three days. It is annoying not to know exactly where Mount Badon was, but we can see it as a hill fort somewhat like Badbury Rings, in a position that would allow Arthur's men to see the Saxons moving southwest and to block their advance. We are entitled to imagine Arthur, warned in advance of this largest of all Saxon attacks, mustering troops from all the southwestern tribes, and using in Roman fashion the tribal warriors as his central infantry and his own cavalry on the flanks.

Nennius' statement that "on a single day 960 men fell in one onslaught of Arthur's, and no one overcame them but himself alone" strikes us as an exaggeration. We can interpret it, however, as a reference to a magnificent achievement of Arthur's cavalry at some point in the battle. A three-day battle can be accepted: a longer one is recorded by Aneirin a century later. Given the determination of the Saxons under Aelle to take the southwest by a single assault, and the at least equal determination of the British to hold their land and drive back the invaders, we can well imagine charges from either side, struggles in which yards rather than miles were gained or lost before each nightfall. From a much later British poet, Gwalchmai, we can get a sense of the battle and its outcome as Arthur experienced it:

> And before him a grim wild welter
> And clash and havoc and tragic death.
> Troop on bloodstained troop, throb on frightened throb,
> Shaft on shining shaft, spear upon spear,
> Fear on deep fear. . . .
>
> .   .   .   .   .
>
> And grey armour and ruin's anguish,
> And corpses heaped by a red-speared lord,
> And England's horde and engagement with it
> And them demolished in the shambles.

At Mount Badon, Britain itself was at stake. The Saxons, perhaps frustrated by British successes in smaller encounters, gambled on one massive thrust to the southwest, and lost. Gildas was writing from direct knowledge when he called Badon "almost the last but not the least" slaughter of the Saxons. The Saxon power was broken. If they were not killed in the battle itself, the three Saxon kings, Aelle, Aesc, and Cerdic, were all dead by 496.

There is no doubt at all about the greatness of Arthur's victory.

In the following years the Saxons were driven back to their coastal territories; Continental sources record that many Saxons left Britain to settle among the Franks, a clear indication that they regarded further advances in Britain as impossible. It is likely that Arthur met with the Saxon kings to arrange peace terms and boundary lines. We can trust Gildas when he speaks of "our present tranquillity" and denounces a generation that grew up in a Britain at peace. Arthur had won for his Britain not merely a battle, but an age of peace that lasted for fifty years.

*   *   *   *   *

According to the *Annales Cambriae*, about twenty years passed between Arthur's triumph at Badon and his death. As far as direct fact about Arthur is concerned, those years are blank. We are thrown back on guesswork.

I cannot see how Britain could have enjoyed such a long peace without, at least at the beginning, a strong single ruler. If Ambrosius lived long enough to know of the victory at Badon, he was certainly dead soon afterwards. Who was there to succeed him but Arthur? It has often been pointed out that early sources do not refer to Arthur as a king; Nennius, though he calls Ambrosius "king of the British kings," refers only to "Arthur the soldier." On the other hand, a poem on Gereint ab Erbin, the seventh-century Cornish ruler, refers to Arthur as "ameraudur," a Celtic word that comes from the Latin "imperator," emperor. It is a thin basis on which to build, but there were, as we have seen, earlier British generals proclaimed emperor by their troops. Ambrosius may well have avoided such titles as "king" and "emperor," preferring that of "vicar"; by 495, any hope for a single Roman Empire must have vanished, since the Continent was now divided into Germanic kingdoms under the Visigoths, the Ostrogoths (in control of Rome itself), the Burgundians, and, in Gaul, the Franks. Under such conditions, for Arthur to follow in the path of earlier leaders and assume the title "Emperor of Britain" would have been natural and even proper. Arguments over words can be useless. Whatever his title may have been, I think that Arthur was in fact ruler of Britain: we may just as well follow later traditions and call him King Arthur, for he would have held the rank of High King.

There is an old saying that "a peaceful nation has no history." It is violence that makes headlines now and was recorded by chronicles then, but not the least of Arthur's achievements may have been peaceful ones. I am only guessing, with no evidence at all except the negative evidence of nothing "important" happening, no serious outbreak of war within the kingdom or threat of invasion, but I think that Arthur followed the examples of his predecessor Ambrosius and of Agricola centuries earlier. As far as he could do so, I believe he attempted to keep Britain united by preventing tribal warfare, by seeing to it that the kingdom was justly governed, and by fostering the life of the mind and the spirit.

Whatever he thought of it, he could hardly prevent the kingdom from becoming increasingly Celtic. The towns continued to fall into decay through disuse, and there was no means of restoring them and no reason to do so. We simply do not know much about the villas during the early sixth century. Some of them probably continued to be used, but more as the estates of Celtic lords than of Roman gentlemen; many probably became the sites of Celtic villages, with the great houses abandoned or ransacked for building materials.

I cannot see Arthur using a town as his center of government, or a villa for that matter. If Cadbury had been suitable for his headquarters as a general, it would have been equally suitable for his center of government. Marriage to the daughter of a tribal king would have been politically wise, and on that unromantic basis, at least, we can believe that he married, perhaps even before his victory at Badon, Gwenhwyfar, more familiar to us as Guenevere. But I cannot see Arthur becoming altogether "Celtic." There is an inscribed cross from seventh-century Gwynedd that pays tribute to *Catamanus rex, sapientisimus, opimatisimus omnium regum*, King Cadfan, most learned, most renowned of all kings. Is it too much to suggest that Arthur was also *sapiens*, a man interested in learning? It is of interest, too, that Gildas refers to such government officials as *rectores*, regional governors, and *speculatores*, the governors' executive officers, when he complains that the civil rulers can no longer control the warfaring lords. This suggests that Arthur had strengthened rather than weakened Roman forms of government.

One major source of intellectual and spiritual life flourished during Arthur's reign, British monasticism. Whether or not Arthur encouraged this, it could not have developed as it did without the peace and freedom he won for the Britons. The sixth century is known as "The Age of the Saints" in Britain and Ireland; "saint" was a word of broader meaning then, and referred to a man who had dedicated his life to religion. The most important of these men was Illtud, who lived at the same time as Arthur. Illtud, trained in Gaul, earned the reputation of "teacher of the Britons," and at his monastic community, Llanilltud, men received both religious and secular education, studying grammar, rhetoric, philosophy, and mathematics, as well as Scripture and theology. Illtud's disciples traveled throughout the southwest and overseas to Brittany, establishing their own monastic communities; the most famous of them is David, who became patron saint of Wales. It was to these British monasteries that the Irish came in the early sixth century, during and after Arthur's reign. We know far more about the Irish monastic communities than about the British, but it is fair to assume that the Irish continued and developed the traditions they had learned through their studies in Britain. The Irish monastic schools were open to laymen, the sons of landowners, as well as to future monks. In general, pagan literature, both classical and native, was not rejected but was accepted for its moral and literary values. The spiritual quality of monastic Christianity at its best can be seen in a passage from an Irish sermon on St. Paul: "Every man's sickness was his own sickness, offence to any man was offence to him, every man's weakness was his own weakness. In the same way it is proper for each of us to suffer with every man in his hardship and in his poverty and in his weakness. We see from the words and wisdom of this learned man that sharing another's suffering is one kind of cross."

Arthur could easily have visited Llanilltud. If he did indeed have his royal hall at Cadbury, he could even more easily have visited the monastic community at nearby Ynys Afallon, later known as Glastonbury. Stories centuries afterwards constantly linked Arthur's name with Glastonbury, but it is hard to know how far to trust these.

Many later stories present an Arthur hostile to the church, and this calls for some explanation. The Arthur of Nennius and the *Annales Cambriae* is not anti-Christian: on the contrary, he carries the image of the Virgin or of the Cross, probably on his shield, and is portrayed as the defender of Christian Britain against pagan invaders. The later stories come mostly from quite legendary lives of the Celtic saints, and show a regular pattern; in each case, Arthur commits some offense, is rebuked by the saint, and then does penance. This tells us nothing of the real Arthur: it shows only that because of his fame he could be used to demonstrate how secular power yielded to the spiritual power of the particular saint.

Silence from Gildas is sometimes a blessing. If Arthur had been an unjust ruler, if he had used his considerable wealth and power against the church, we would certainly have heard of him from Gildas. Instead, Gildas, in denouncing the laymen and the clergy of his own time, implies that earlier in the century the tribal rulers were kept in check and the country governed firmly and justly. That part of the century was the age of Arthur. Gildas, the more we study him, seems to be in the odd position of a man who does not even wish to mention Arthur because he is reluctant to praise him, but whose every comment on Britain after the victory at Badon implies the presence of a strong and wise High King.

In its entry for the year 537, the *Annales Cambriae* says simply: "The Battle of Camlann, in which Arthur and Medraut fell." The date, as usual, is too late: Arthur, born about 460, probably died about 520. This gives us very little, but it can be accepted as fact. From later traditions, we can trust only a little: Medraut as the leader of a revolt against Arthur we can believe; Medraut as Arthur's nephew is less likely.

We have a record of one Medrawt who lived at exactly the right time. He was a grandson of King Caradawc of Gwent, but he was not the ruler of that kingdom. So we have a second fact—and that is all. Back to guesswork: I think that Arthur's belief in a united Britain, shared by most of the tribal lords when the need for union was clear, was not shared by some of those born in the peaceful era his policies had achieved. Gildas is very clear about this: a generation has grown up that never knew the dangers that threatened their fathers, and these lords are going back to tribal thinking and tribal warfare. We can imagine that Medraut, punished or even exiled for such warfare by Iddon, his king, at Arthur's insistence, gathered an army of rebels and attacked Arthur's own region. Possibly some truth lies behind the tales of Medraut's capturing Arthur's fortress and holding Guenevere captive while the king himself was elsewhere and suspected nothing. All we can say with any certainty is that there was a battle in which both men were killed; where it took place, we do not know.

In 1190, what is supposed to have been the grave of Arthur was opened at Glastonbury Abbey. Adam of Domerham, a monk of the abbey, wrote one hundred years later that the abbot, Henry de Sully, was "frequently urged to dispose more fittingly of the famous king (for he had lain for 648 years near the old church between two pyramids, at one time splendidly carved). One day he had the place surrounded by curtains and gave orders for the excavation. . . . The Abbot and the monks, lifting out the remains, brought them with joy into the great church, laying them in a double tomb." This tomb was opened in 1278 by Edward I, and according to Adam, "the bones of the king were of great size." A chronicler, Geraldus Cambrensis, visited the abbey in 1192, was shown Arthur's tomb, and wrote the story of the discovery. He claims particularly to have seen "a lead cross, placed under a stone and not over it, as is now the custom. . . . I have felt the letters engraved on it, which do not stand out but are indented. . . . They read as follows: Here Lies Buried The Renowned King Arthur With Guenevere His Second Wife In The Island Of Avalon." The tomb at Glastonbury and the bones in it were destroyed during the English Reformation, in the sixteenth century.

Ynys Afallon (the Island of Apples), with its small monastic settlement and church, would have been an appropriate burial place for Arthur. Celtic rulers were often honored by being buried in monastic graveyards. If Arthur really lived at Cadbury and was mortally wounded in battle near there, and if he had been a patron of the monastery and a worshipper in its church, such a grave would have been especially fitting. What is bothersome is the apparent secrecy of the burial, and the long years in which no one except the monks of Glastonbury knew the site of Arthur's grave. Explanations are possible. It may have been politically desirable to keep Arthur's death a secret, especially from the Saxons, and later events would not have encouraged the monks to reveal the grave to Saxon conquerors. Archeologists have recently investigated the grave-site; the results lead us to believe that a person of some importance was buried exactly where the monks said he was, and that the burial took place around Arthur's time. But I still have some doubts.

It was politically very convenient for the King, Henry II, to crush the Celtic prophecies that Arthur would return and lead them to victory, by proving that Arthur had been dead for centuries. Henry could then claim that his own Normans had carried out Arthur's mission to defeat the English, and so justify his possession of Arthur's throne. It seems significant that Henry's grandson was named Arthur: it was clearly hoped that he would become Arthur II, a hope that died when young Arthur did, at the hands of King John.

What really matters is not where Arthur was buried but when, where, and how he lived. We can accept or reject the evidence from Glastonbury that he was an unusually large man, but we shall still never know his exact appearance. Is it so important? At the end of Tacitus' biography of Agricola, the young man who was to become ruler of Britain would have read the following words: "The image of the human face, like the face itself, is fragile and fades away, but the spirit's essence lasts forever. It can never be captured and shown by a stranger's tools and skill; you alone can show it by your own way of life. Everything in Agricola that earned our affection and admiration lives on and will continue to live on in the hearts of men." So it was to be with Arthur; I think he would have been satisfied. He would surely have been pleased, too, by the words of William of Malmesbury, a fitting epitaph: "For a long time he gave strength to his weakened homeland, and revived the broken spirits of his countrymen."

4

The Fall of the Kingdom

Though there are a few references to Arthur's having a son, in all the stories he dies childless. The tradition that the rule of Britain passed to Constantine, king of Cornwall, may well be true. The dates are right: Constantine is one of the rulers denounced by Gildas, and it is noteworthy that he is accused of murdering Medraut's sons. Gildas does not name anyone as sole ruler of Britain; he does imply that some kind of central government continued, though it was less and less able to hold the kingdom together.

Britain was to enjoy about thirty years of comparative peace after Arthur's death. As of 550, most of the island was still under British rule. By 600, only a few isolated kingdoms in the west and north were ruled by Britons. Those fifty years saw the end of Britain, and the foundation of England.

One reason for the collapse of Arthur's Britain was a lack of Christian charity. This may seem a strange statement when I have just noted the flourishing of British Christianity in the early sixth century, particularly through the growth of the monasteries. But the British missionaries of that period concentrated on Britain itself and on Ireland and Brittany—we hear of no attempt to convert the Saxons. That does not mean that none was made, but the contrast with the intense and successful Irish missions to the Saxons in the next century forces us to one conclusion: the leaders of the British Church were more British than Christian in their treatment of the Saxons.

Excuses can be found. For one thing, there was abundant mis-

sionary work to be done among the Scots and Picts, as well as among the Britons, Irish, and Bretons. For another, the Saxons were of all the Germanic tribes the least "civilized" or "Romanized," the least likely to accept, as the Franks did in 496, the Christian religion. The British Church in either the sixth or the early seventh century issued a stern warning against treason: "To any who give assistance to the barbarians, 13 years penance if there has been no slaughter of Christians or spilling of blood or harsh captivity. But if such things do happen, the sinners shall do penance, and lay down their arms for the rest of their lives. But if someone plotted to lead the barbarians to the Christians, and did this deliberately, he must do penance for the remainder of his life." Not for the first or the last time in history, Christianity and patriotism seem to have become one. The Saxons had threatened to extinguish both the nation and its religion through most of the fifth century: the effects were natural enough, and long-lasting. The Celtic bishops of Britain refused to aid St. Augustine in his mission to the English at the end of the sixth century; one bishop is supposed to have remarked that "if the Saxons go to heaven, heaven itself would be unbearable." It is all quite understandable—and by the standards of Christianity itself, deplorable. When all excuses have been made, we must still say that the British failed to live their faith.

We cannot be sure that British missionary efforts among the Saxons would have had any success, or that conversion would have prevented the Saxon conquest of Britain. But I, for one, would welcome some evidence that the Britons at least tried.

If we are to give Arthur credit for encouraging the growth of British Christianity, then he must share with the abbots and bishops of his time the blame for this spiritual failure and its political effects. But the major cause of Britain's collapse was tribalism, and, if my view of Arthur is correct, he was its lifelong opponent and finally its victim. Peter Abrahams' analysis of modern Africa is again useful to us: he says of "tribal man" that "his society is exclusive and not, like western society, inclusive. The lines are drawn very clearly, very sharply. Anybody not an 'insider' is an enemy, actually or potentially—someone to distrust, someone to fear, someone to keep at bay. There is no choice, no volition about this. It is something ordained by the ancestral dead. . . . If you are not in the tribe, there is no way into it. If you are in it, there is no way out except death." Abrahams adds that tribal man "will have a crucial say in the future of Africa." Tribal man had a crucial say in the future of Arthur's Britain. If you think I am wrong to compare modern Africa and sixth-century Britain, let me note that at this moment, as I am writing of the destruction of that Britain, Nigeria is being torn apart by what is basically a tribal war. And it occurs to me that we can find "tribal thinking" going on even closer to home.

With Arthur dead, there was no ruler powerful enough or farsighted enough to prevent the gradual breaking of the kingdom into tribal groups. Gildas denounces five rulers for a variety of offences; he is not an impartial witness, but we can believe him when he speaks of their constant warfare against each other. The five kings are Constantine of Dumnonia; Aurelius Caninus, a descendant of Ambrosius Aurelianus, who ruled the region of the Dobunni; Voteporix of Dyfed; Cynglas of Ceredigion; and Maelgwn of Gwynedd. Of the five, Gildas plainly regarded Maelgwn as the most powerful. He is described as surpassing all the others in his size, his generosity, and his skill in war. Gildas states that Maelgwn had studied under Illtud, and, despite the vices he is accused of, the picture that emerges is of a very energetic, intelligent, and cultivated Celtic ruler—but the ruler of a tribe, not a nation. The five rulers are significantly the leaders of those regions of Britain that had played the greatest part in the defeat of the Saxons. There is no evidence that their tribal quarrels allowed the Saxons to advance, but they foreshadow what was to come. When the Saxons did break the long peace, there was no single ruler who could unite the Britons against them.

I have given two major causes for the collapse of Britain: there was a third. An epidemic, the Yellow Plague, spread from Persia to the continent of Europe, and through Brittany was carried to Britain. The British suffered severely; the Saxons were less affected. In 547, Maelgwn of Gwynedd died of the plague. A few years later, against the weakened and divided British, the Saxons began to move.

*   *   *   *   *

It was Cynric, Cerdic's grandson, who gave Wessex the leadership Britain lacked. In 552, according to the *Anglo-Saxon Chronicle,* "Cynric fought against the Britons in the place which is called Salisbury, and put the Britons to flight." Four years later, Cynric and his son Ceawlin defeated the British further north, possibly near the site of Mount Badon. The region Ambrosius and Arthur had succeeded in holding sixty years before fell quickly into Saxon hands.

Ceawlin became king of Wessex in 560, and earned the title of *Bretwalda,* ruler of Britain, in a series of victories. The most important battle was in 577 at Dyrham, after which the Saxons "captured three of their cities, Gloucester, Cirencester, and Bath." It is doubtful that the cities were still inhabited at this time; the chronicler is indicating the region by using the town names. This had been, remember, the region of Ambrosius and Arthur, the strongest and most civilized part of Britain in the fifth and early sixth centuries. There was British resistance: Dyrham was the site of an ancient hill fort, which was presumably used as Arthur had used Badon; three British kings, "Conmail, Condidan, and Farinmail," were killed. However hard they may have fought, the British suffered a decisive defeat. The Saxons now held the south from the east coast to the Bristol Channel. The southwestern peninsula was still under British rule, but it was now cut off from the rest of Britain.

We know very little of how the midland area came into Saxon hands, except that it happened. Some of the settlement may have been by comparatively peaceful migration westwards. There was intermarriage between the ruling Saxons and the conquered Celts in the eastern kingdoms, and we need not think of Celt and Saxon as forever or everywhere at each other's throats.

There was stronger resistance in the north, but here again, it was tribalism that defeated the British. In 575, Rhydderch of Strathclyde won a great victory—but against other Celtic rulers, not against the English. It was because of this battle that Rhydderch's chief bard, Myrddin (Merlin), is said to have gone mad and to have taken to living as a savage in the forest. On the northeast coast, the English had occupied the small kingdoms of Deira and Bernicia at some time early in the sixth century. The *Chronicle* notes that in 547 "Ida, from whom the royal family of the Northumbrians took its rise, succeeded to the kingdom. And he reigned twelve years; and he built Bamburgh, which was first enclosed with a hedge and afterwards with a wall." If these northeastern English kingdoms expanded before the last decade of the sixth century, they did so very slowly. They were almost, at one point, eliminated completely. An alliance of northern British kings under Urien of Rheged drove the king of Bernicia to take refuge on the island of Lindisfarne sometime around 580. But the alliance did not last; the Britons quarrelled, and Urien was killed by another British ruler, Morgant.

The condition of the British is reflected in the poems of Taliesin, composed between 575 and 590. In one, Taliesin praises Cynan, ruler of Powys, for his success in battles with Gwent, Gwynedd, and Dyfed, and calls him a threat to Cornwall. There is not a hint that Cynan fought anyone but his fellow Britons. Taliesin became Urien of Rheged's court bard, and his poems show Urien and his son Owain in battles with the Picts and the northern Britons as well as with the English. It is for a victory over the English, however, that Taliesin praises Owain in lamenting the prince's death. The impression given by Taliesin's work is of British kings thinking only in tribal terms, fighting with each other at a time when their survival depended on joining against the English. In one of Taliesin's poems, the fort near the important crossroads at Catraeth, modern Catterick, is in British hands; ten years or so later, a poem by Aneirin shows that it had been captured by the English.

In 593, Aethelfrith became king of Bernicia, and it was probably under his leadership that Catraeth fell to the English. Aethelfrith formed an alliance with the kingdom of Deira, determined to conquer the northern British kingdoms, and the Britons at last responded to their danger. In what seems to be a deliberate imitation of Arthur's methods, Mynyddawg, king of Gododdin, assembled a cavalry force of about three hundred men at Din Eidin (Edinburgh). The warriors came not only from Gododdin but from the other northern and the southern British kingdoms as well. After a period of intensive training and lavish feasts, they rode on the long road south to attack the fortress at Catraeth. Once more it was British cavalry against English foot-soldiers, but the English greatly outnumbered the British and held a strongly fortified position. In a week of fighting, all but a few of the Britons were killed. Aneirin, the court bard of Gododdin, survived the battle; he chanted of the courage of the war-band and the bitterness of defeat:

> Men went to Catraeth, keen their war-band;
> Pale mead their portion, it was poison;
> Three hundred under orders to fight.
> And after celebration, silence.
> Though they went to churches for shriving,
> True is the tale, death confronted them.
>
> .   .   .   .
>
> Men launched the assault, moving as one,
> A war-band steadfast in battle, shields shattered.
> And though they were being slain, they slew.
> Not one to his own region returned.
>
> .   .   .   .
>
> Warriors rose together, formed ranks:
> With a single mind they assaulted.
> Short their lives, long their kinsmen long for them.
> Seven times their sum of English they slew.
> Their fighting turned wives into widows;
> Many a mother with tear-filled eyelids.
>
> .   .   .   .

And long the moaning and the mourning
For the countryside's stalwart soldiers,
At the hardest posts, staunch under stress.
May their souls be, after the battle,
Welcomed to heaven's land of plenty.

The Britons had combined for a valiant, last-ditch effort, and it failed. We know of no other major battle in the north, and no wonder, since the finest British warriors must have fallen at Catraeth. When next we hear of Aethelfrith, he has won a great victory in 603 over Aedan, king of the Scots of Dalriata, and is in control of the entire northeast of Britain to the borders of Pictland. In 616, Aethelfrith in one swift stroke cut off what remained of the northern kingdoms, destroying a British army at Chester. Rheged and Elmet seem to have been gradually occupied by the English without serious resistance. Only Strathclyde remained a British kingdom; it stubbornly kept its independence for the next four hundred years.

There was one British attempt to recover the north, a savage counterattack by Cadwallon of Gwynedd, striking with brief success far into what was now Northumbria. But with the defeat and death of Cadwallon in 633, Britain was no more. Now there were only the small and isolated British kingdoms of Strathclyde, of Cornwall, of the warring tribes in what the English called Wales. There were Pictland and Dalriata, but these had never belonged to the kingdom of Britain. Otherwise, there was England.

* * * * *

Language sometimes preserves a moment of history. During the years after 550, the Britons began to refer to themselves as *Cymry*, fellow countrymen. This is what the Welsh still call themselves in their own language. At the same time, the English began to use a word of their own for the Britons. The modern form of the word is "Welsh." It meant "foreigners."

5

Voices and Visions

The real Arthur, the Arthur of history, soon became the Arthur of legend. It was bound to happen. There is something of the Poet in all of us; we all hunger for heroes. Think of Washington and Lincoln, of Churchill, of the Kennedys. Even in a "realistic" age, even when historical documents exist in abundance, we persist in seeing certain men not only as they were, but as we want them to have been, and we enlarge whatever greatness they actually had.

The Celtic bards must have sung of Arthur even while he lived. In the centuries after his death, the Britons of Wales, Cornwall, and Brittany cherished his memory, and their stories of him wove fact and fiction together. There were tales about Arthur voyaging to the "other world," the Celtic fairyland, in search of a magic cauldron, about Arthur hunting a gigantic boar from Ireland to south Wales to Cornwall. Both stories were folk tales popular in Britain and Ireland before Arthur was born, but making Arthur the hero could now give new interest to an old story. In the same way, characters became more glamorous if they were made members of Arthur's court. Myrddin (Merlin), the court-poet of King Rhydderch of Strathclyde in the later sixth century; Geraint, the Dumnonian king killed by the Saxons after 600; Tristan, originally a Pictish hero; Peredur and Gwalchmai, two northern British warriors of the late sixth century better known to us as Perceval and Gawain—all became part of the growing legend of Arthur. Of the characters who appear in later stories, only Guenevere, Mordred, Kay, and Bedivere were probably really present in Arthur's great hall.

It was a poet posing as a historian, Geoffrey of Monmouth, who first put together the various legends of Arthur. Geoffrey's father was named Arthur, and he was partly Welsh; as a young boy, he would have heard tales of King Arthur. His *Historia Regum Britanniae (A History of the Kings of Britain)* appeared in 1136; in the preface, Geoffrey claims that he is merely translating into Latin "a very old book in the British language." No one now believes this. Even in his own century, William of Newburgh accused Geoffrey of having "disguised under the respectable name of history the fables about Arthur which he took from the ancient fictions of the Britons and added to out of his own head." That says it pretty well: Geoffrey takes whatever suits him from Gildas and Nennius, and works in bits and pieces from Celtic poems and stories; how much comes "out of his own head" we cannot tell. The result is certainly not history, but it is a good story, good enough to be read for centuries in Europe as well as England and Wales. Geoffrey's version of Arthur's life became the basis for most later poems and stories.

As his title shows, Geoffrey wrote of other British rulers, but the largest portion of his book was devoted to Arthur. Geoffrey presents Ambrosius and Uther Pendragon as brothers, with Uther becoming the father of Arthur by the aid of Merlin the wizard. Arthur is born in the Cornish castle of Tintagel, and becomes at fifteen the ruler of Britain. With a sword called Caliburn, forged in the Isle of Avallon, he defeats not only the Saxons but the Scots and the Picts. After marrying Ganhumara, "a wife born of a noble Roman family," Arthur goes on to conquer Ireland, Iceland, Norway, Gaul, and Gothland. He establishes a splendid court at Caerleon; Britain under his rule surpasses "all other kingdoms in abundance of riches, in luxury of adornment, and in the courteous wit of those who dwelt in it. Whatever knight in the land was famed for his prowess wore his clothing and his arms all of one single color. And the ladies, no less playful, would dress themselves the same way in a single color, and they scorned to have the love of any man who had not proved himself three times in battle. And therefore in those days ladies became more chaste and knights became more noble because of their love. "

When Lucius, Emperor of Rome, demands Arthur's submission, Arthur gathers his army and marches against Rome. (Geoffrey has clearly taken the history of Magnus Maximus and given the central role to Arthur!) In the midst of victory, Arthur receives news that his nephew Modred, whom he had left in charge of Britain, has claimed the kingdom and forced Ganhumara to marry him. Arthur defeats Modred in a battle in Cornwall; Modred is killed, and "the renowned King Arthur himself was mortally wounded, and was carried from there to the Isle of Avallon to have his wounds healed, where he gave the crown of Britain to his kinsman, Constantine, Duke of Cornwall, in the year of the Incarnation of Our Lord five hundred and forty-two." After Arthur leaves the scene, the kingdom is ruled successively by Constantine, Aurelius, Vortipore, and Malgo—four kings whom we have seen were actually living at the same time. Under "Careticus, a lover of civil wars," Britain falls into the hands of the Saxons, and so "the Britons lost the crown of the kingdom and the rule over the island."

Arthurian stories had already been spread through the Continent by Breton poets, but Geoffrey's work, well-constructed and well-told, had a powerful and long-lasting impact on artists as well as poets in many countries. In two Italian cathedrals, for example, there are carvings and a mosiac from the late twelfth century portraying Arthur. If we ask why an early British king caught the imaginations of so many people in so many lands throughout the later Middle Ages, the answer lies with Geoffrey. By making Arthur the emperor of most of western Europe, by giving him a magnificent court whose customs were of the twelfth rather than the sixth century, above all by adding touches of magic, love interest, and a tragic betrayal, Geoffrey created an immortal legend, one that has buried for centuries the real achievements of the historical Arthur.

In the year Geoffrey died, 1155, a Norman poet named Wace completed his version of the Arthurian story. Wace's *Roman de Brut* is based on Geoffrey's work, but he expanded the story considerably both by presenting scenes in dramatic detail and by adding material from Breton poets. It is in Wace that we first hear of the Round Table, constructed at Arthur's command so that quarrels could be avoided: "At the table they sat on an equal level and were served equally." And it is in Wace that Arthur has his chosen band of knights, "those of the Round Table, who were praised throughout the world."

Fifty years later, the story was written for the first time in English, the language of Arthur's enemies, by a priest named Layamon. It is odd that Layamon begins his poem *Brut* by declaring that he intends "to tell of the noble deeds of the English"; as we might expect, the noble deeds are performed by the Britons, and the English are the villains. Layamon, like Wace, is a good poet, and he tells vividly the story of Arthur, using Wace as his chief source. He adds a dream in which Arthur foresees the treachery of Modred. But he omits the strong element of love that Wace, taking his cue from Geoffrey, had developed as the knights' chief motive for performing brave deeds. Layamon sees Arthur chiefly in terms of Anglo-Saxon battle poems, not French romances. He does add to the story touches that are Celtic, probably Breton in origin. "Alven" (elves, fairies) bless Arthur at birth with the three gifts of strength, leadership, and long life. Layamon develops what is only hinted at by Geoffrey and mentioned doubtfully by Wace, the legend of Arthur's mysterious departure and promised return:

> "I will voyage to Avalon, to the fairest of maidens,
> To Argante the queen, loveliest elf-lady,
> And she will make healthy all of my wounds,
> And cure me completely with healing potions.
> After that I shall come once more to my kingdom,
> And dwell with the Britons in great delight."
> Even as he spoke there came from the sea
> A small boat gliding, driven by the waves,
> And in it two women marvellously clothed.
> At once they took Arthur, and carried him quickly,
> And set him down gently, and then sailed away.
> The Britons still believe that he is living,
> And dwells in Avalon with the loveliest elf-lady.
> There once was a prophet, Merlin by name,
> Who uttered predictions, his sayings were true,
> That an Arthur should come to aid the Britons.

*   *   *   *   *

It was not English but Continental voices, however, that carried on and added to Arthurian legend. Breton voices at first, then French and German. Chrétien de Troyes wrote his Arthurian poems in the late twelfth century, using Breton stories to explore in French verse the experience of love. In Chrétien's work, Arthur and his court provide the background, but other characters play the major roles. Erec, for instance, is a knight of the Round Table, and he brings his wife Enide to Arthur's court, but the story is essentially about their marital problems. In the story of *Cligès*, the hero's father Alexandre sails from Constantinople to Arthur's court in Britain, and falls in love with Gauvain's sister; his courtship is helped by Guenièvre. Cligès as a young man also visits Arthur's court, where in a tournament he proves himself by defeating Lancelot and Perceval. In *Lancelot* the center of the story is, of course, the hero's adulterous love affair with Guenièvre, and Lancelot's rescue of the queen when she is carried off by Meleagant. In earlier versions of the story, the queen had been rescued by Arthur himself: it was Chrétien who created the love affair that became a central part of Arthur's story. Lancelot du Lac had been brought into Arthurian legend by earlier poets; thanks to Chrétien, he became a major character.

With Chrétien, the emphasis shifts away from Arthur to other characters who had become linked with him. Geoffrey, Wace, and Layamon presented an heroic king who established a just and splendid realm but was betrayed; the characters were clearly drawn and not very complex. Chrétien offered instead stories that were connected with Arthur's court but that seldom involved Arthur's own actions. Arthurian story had been moving in that direction for some time: there are Welsh prose romances that use the same unknown sources as Chrétien. Chrétien was the one, however, who set the course for later writers. He was a master of the short narrative in verse, and he was more interested in the conflicts of a few characters than in the fate of a kingdom. The heroes of his stories struggle to find a balance between the self-fulfillment of love for a lady and the self-denial demanded by their duties as knights. They are individual human beings trying to live up to the ideals that Chrétien assumes are those of Arthur's Britain, and they sometimes fail.

Chrétien writes tales that are complete in themselves but that make one ask how they fit into the total Arthurian story. This, at least, is how some later writers felt, and they set themselves the task of pulling the pieces together. One way to do this was by using the story of the Holy Grail.

*   *   *   *   *

Although we should probably give Chrétien the credit for making the Grail important in Arthurian legend, he was not the first to tell the story, and his *Perceval* is a much less developed and successful poem than Wolfram von Eschenbach's *Parzival*, composed in German between 1200 and 1210. Wolfram has his own voice and his own vision, and neither is the same as Chrétien's, even though he based his poem on *Perceval*. Wolfram, like Chrétien, presents us with the adventures of two knights of Arthur's court, Parzival and Gawan, but he adds a fresh and critical view of Arthur's Britain. He sees it as an example of the best that man can do for himself. Gawan typifies the Arthurian values of courage and courtesy, but this way of life lacks the completeness and joy man gains by dedicating himself to God and receiving divine grace. The community of the Grail, with its spiritual values that Parzival gradually learns, is placed by Wolfram in direct contrast to Arthur's noble but worldly court.

Other voices, other visions, especially of the Grail itself. For Chrétien, the Grail was a platter that held a consecrated wafer, and it was used to feed one holy invalid. For Wolfram, the Grail was a sacred stone that could provide every man with whatever food and drink he wished; the sight of it made men youthful and long-lived. For Robert de Boron, the Grail was the cup Christ blessed at the Last Supper; in it, Joseph of Arimathea caught the last drops of Christ's blood when He was crucified. Robert has Joseph found an Order of the Grail: those who belong to it must lead pure lives, and when they sit at the Grail table, they receive all that they desire. According to Robert, the Grail was brought to "Avaron," Glastonbury.

After Robert, there were a number of stories in which a quest for the Grail became a test of the virtues of Arthur and his chief knights. I cannot go into all of these, and there is no need to do so. What is important is that a new vision of Arthur's Britain comes into being, one in which the knights' adventures become efforts to achieve sanctity.

I must comment, however, on a remarkable series of prose stories,

Lancelot, Queste del Saint Graal, and *Mort Artu,* written between 1215 and 1230. In these, three unknown French authors attempt, with considerable success, to shape the various tales of earlier writers into one meaningful and unified story. The narrative begins by concentrating on Lancelot, a king's son who is kidnapped and raised by the elvish Lady of the Lake. She instructs him in the duties of knighthood, particularly the need to use his gifts as a warrior for the protection of the weak and the defense of Holy Church rather than to satisfy his own desires and pride. When Lancelot is eighteen, she brings him to Arthur's court, where he is knighted and where he falls in love with the queen. A series of adventures follows in which Lancelot gains the reputation of being Arthur's best knight and also wins the love of Guenièvre. As he rises in worldly reputation, however, he loses some of his finer qualities, treating his opponents without the mercy he had earlier shown and sinning by his affair with the queen. In visits to the castle of Pelles, keeper of the Grail, three of Arthur's knights, Gauvain, Bohort, and Lancelot, are tested. The Grail is seen by all three: Gauvain, judged completely unworthy, receives no food from the magic chalice, is wounded in his sleep by a magic lance, and exits in disgrace, carried in a cart; Bohort has some of the same experiences, but is judged worthy to learn some of the Grail's mysteries; Lancelot is not humiliated as Gauvain is, but he does not receive the privileges given to Bohort.

While it is clear to Guenièvre that Lancelot's failure has been caused by their adultery, Lancelot himself refuses to believe it. Pelles arranges to have his daughter sleep with Lancelot, who is bewitched by a potion into thinking he is making love to Guenièvre: from this union, Galaad is born. Guenièvre, jealous, rejects Lancelot; he goes out of his mind, but is finally cured by the Grail. When Galaad as a young man is received at Arthur's court, the Grail appears in a brilliant light, floating from table to table and serving each man with the food he most wishes, and then disappears. The knights make a vow to go in quest of the Grail, and the story follows a number of them through varied adventures. Most of them do not really understand the meaning of the quest, and such knights as Lionel and Gauvain fail in the enterprise and return to court. Lancelot has gained wisdom: he confesses his guilt to a hermit, does penance, and is therefore permitted an experience of spiritual joy at the Grail Castle before he must return to Arthur's court. Three knights alone, Bohort, Perceval, and Galaad, succeed in the quest, though Bohort and Perceval suffer from temptations that do not affect Galaad. All three are present when Christ himself ascends from the Grail and serves communion; all three sail in Solomon's ship to the land of Sarras, where Galaad sees plainly the ultimate vision within the Grail and dies in a state of intense joy. A hand then takes the Grail to heaven. Perceval dies a year later; Bohort returns to Arthur's court at Camaalot to tell the story.

After the Grail quest is over, life at Arthur's court resumes. Lancelot once again becomes Guenièvre's lover, not without torments of conscience, and Arthur begins to grow suspicious. When the lovers are caught together and Guenièvre is sentenced to be burned at the stake, Lancelot rescues her, killing Gauvain's brother in the struggle. Arthur lays siege to Lancelot's castle, Joyeuse Garde; when the Pope intercedes, Arthur takes Guenièvre back, and Lancelot sails to his own kingdom overseas. Arthur and Gauvain bring an army against Lancelot, but when Lancelot wounds Gauvain, the army withdraws. At this point the Romans invade France; after defeating them, Arthur learns that Mordret has rebelled and returns to Britain. (Mordret in this story is Arthur's own son, born of Arthur's incest with his sister.) Gauvain dies of his wounds, sending a last message asking Lancelot's forgiveness; Arthur kills Mordret in battle, but is mortally wounded himself. He is carried away by ladies in a boat; his tomb is discovered several days later. Guenièvre repents and becomes a nun; Lancelot, after killing Mordret's sons in battle, becomes a hermit. At his death, Lancelot's soul is carried to heaven by angels.

We have come a long way, obviously, not only from the historical Arthur but from Geoffrey of Monmouth. Despite some faults, the unknown authors have drawn into a unified story many of the earlier tales. Their voices present a single vision suggested by earlier works but not fully developed: Arthur's Britain is the world of varied humanity, with all its faults and its virtues, called by divine grace to perfection but failing often to answer the call. At the center is Lancelot rather than Arthur, a tragic hero who develops from a valiant but untroubled sinner into a penitent seeker of perfection, slips back into sin but acknowledges not only his personal guilt but his and Guenièvre's responsibility for the collapse of the kingdom, and dies as a remorseful man forgiven by a merciful God.

These three linked works, usually referred to as a single book, the "Prose *Lancelot*," had an enormous popularity in the next centuries. Later Arthurian stories—not only in France but also in Italy, Spain, Portugal, the Netherlands, and England—were strongly influenced by it; the *Queste* section was translated into Irish and Welsh; Dante referred to it several times in his *Divine Comedy*. As a modern critic has said, "it is not the most perfect work of romance and mysticism medieval France produced, but it was certainly the most powerful."

*   *   *   *   *

I do not care to trace all the developments of Arthurian story through the later Middle Ages, and I doubt that you would want me to. So I shall say nothing about such matters as Dutch and Scandinavian romances of Arthur except that they existed and show how popular the stories had become. Back we go to England. Even among the medieval English stories in verse and prose, I shall comment only on those that still make good reading and that show individual vision. That leaves us with three works—the alliterative poem *Morte Arthure*, *Sir Gawain and the Green Knight*, and the book by Sir Thomas Malory that has usually been known as *Morte d'Arthur*.

The unknown author of the alliterative *Morte Arthure* composed his poem around 1360. What is most interesting about it, apart from its moments of great poetry, is the poet's refusal to follow the pattern set by the French. Instead he returns to Geoffrey of Monmouth, and Arthur is once more the central character. He emphasizes the end of the story, Arthur's victory over the Roman emperor and the treason of Mordred. He is not interested in love affairs or fairyland or the quest for sanctity. This poet creates a warrior Arthur, who is human in his deep affection for his knights and his heartbroken grief when Gawain is slain in battle by Mordred, and who dies with quiet dignity at Glastonbury.

The author is more interested in the king than in the kingdom, and this is why he limits himself to the later part of the story. His vision stresses how short-lived and perishable human greatness and power are. We see Arthur rejoice in his victory over Rome, then watch as he learns of Mordred's betrayal. There is throughout the poem the sense that those who rise to greatness will sooner or later fall, because that is the way things are. It is true that Arthur is told after his ominous dream that he is guilty of pride and of shedding innocent men's blood in warfare, and Arthur does say that his sin caused Gawain's death. We have no strong feeling, however, that Arthur is really much to blame. If a man is a great warrior and king, then this is what is bound to happen to him.

Sir Gawain and the Green Knight, a poem written around 1375, presents a very different Arthur in a very different Britain. Arthur is young, the boyish and boisterous King of a gracious, laughter-loving, devoutly Christian court. Into the great hall during the Christmas feast rides a huge green knight on a green horse to challenge any knight there to a "beheading game." When Arthur, stung by the scornful remarks of the knight, volunteers, Gawain politely but firmly insists on taking his place. The knight is beheaded by Gawain's blow but rises, mounts his horse, and rides from the hall head in hand, after reminding Gawain that he has promised to submit to a similar blow in a year and a day at "the Green Chapel." When spring, summer, and autumn have passed, Gawain sets out on his journey, suffering from bitter winter weather amid the mountains of north Wales before he finds shelter at a splendid castle.

He spends three days at the castle, where he is most cordially welcomed and assured that he will be guided to the Green Chapel on the appointed day. Gawain agrees to his host's proposal that they exchange what they have won at the end of each day, and for three days, as the lord of the castle goes hunting, the lord's wife tempts Gawain in his bedroom. Gawain is courteous but chaste; his only failure comes when the lady gives him a supposedly magic belt that will protect him from physical harm, and he does not exchange this with his host. True to his word, he presents himself before the Green Knight, and bows his head to receive the blow from the axe. The Knight twice deliberately turns the axe aside at the last moment, a nerve-wracking experience for Gawain; on the third swing, he nicks Gawain's neck. The Knight then reveals that he had been the lord of the castle where Gawain was tempted, and that Gawain has proved himself truly noble except for the single failure. Gawain does not forgive himself for yielding as easily as the Knight does; he accuses himself of having been untrue to his word because of his cowardice. He

wears the belt on his return to Arthur's court as a mark of his
disgrace; the court refuses to accept Gawain's verdict on himself,
and each knight wears a similar belt as a sign of honor, not disgrace.

This bare summary can give you nothing of the quality of the
poem, its beauty, wit, and strongly dramatic scenes. Read it, please:
it is one of the finest short narratives in the English language. What
I wish to note here is that the poet, far more effectively than
Chrétien de Troyes had done, makes Gawain's experience a revela-
tion and a testing of the values of Arthur's Britain. Every incident
in the poem is really a test of Gawain's five virtues—generosity,
love for his fellow men, chastity, courtesy, and piety. Gawain's
first action in the story is to risk his life for his king's sake; his last
is to tell the court honestly the story of his failure. His faithful-
ness to his promise is constantly tested: he must find his way to
the unknown Green Chapel; he must endure the hardships of the
journey; he is given a final opportunity to escape by the guide
who brings him to the chapel. Both his chastity and his courtesy
are severely tested by the lady: he must refuse her, but very very
politely! He is all but perfect, yet he is very much a human being:
he does not volunteer for the beheading game until it is necessary
to prevent Arthur from risking his life; he bravely faces what he
believes to be certain death, but he is thoroughly irritated by the
Green Knight's prolonging of the agony; he has the virtue to
refuse the lady, but he does not find it easy. He is all too human
in failing to live up to his ideals when the chance to live is offered
unexpectedly. The author's awareness of human nature is shrewd,
for Gawain is offered this temptation when he is off his guard, at
the very moment when he has with difficulty overcome the temptation to be unchaste. In his own eyes, his single failure is a betrayal
of all his ideals:

> I being craven about our encounter, cowardice
> Connived with covetousness to corrupt my nature
> And the liberality and loyalty belonging to chivalry.
> Now I am faulty and false and found fearful always.

The Green Knight sees it otherwise:

> In my view you have made amends for your misdemeanour;
> You have acknowledged your faults fully in fair confession,

And plainly done penance at the point of my axe.
You are absolved of your sin and as stainless now
As if you had never fallen in fault since first you were born.

The poet's vision of Arthur's court presents an almost ideal human community, highly civilized and deeply Christian. "Almost" is the key word. It needs to be tested by exposure to the strange and uncontrollable elements in life, so that it like Gawain can be made aware that it can fail, that it has not yet achieved perfection. The pleasures of the good life cannot be taken for granted; they must be earned by the readiness to risk not only comfort but life itself, and by the willingness to confess imperfection.

Sir Thomas Malory, in the fifteenth century, wrote what became the most popular English version of the Arthurian story. It might be better to say "versions" and "stories." Malory was concerned less with writing a single long work, a prose "epic" of Arthur, than with telling a series of tales. One of Malory's chief sources was the French "Prose *Lancelot*," but he deliberately separated that imperfect but unified narrative into individual stories. There is some pattern in the arrangement of his book: Malory begins with Arthur's victory over the Emperor of Rome, which, as we have seen, was Arthur's last triumph in other versions, and he ends with the civil war that destroyed Arthur's Britain; in between, he places the individual adventures of various knights in a Britain that enjoys the generally peaceful reign of a wise, just, and benevolent king. To claim more unity than this would, I think, be wrong, though there are those who disagree.

At his best, Malory is a fine storyteller; at his worst, he is just plain dull. Such stories as "The Tale of Gareth" and "The Fair Maid of Astolat" are excellent; the long retelling of the story of Tristan is not. If you are wondering why I have said so little of Tristan before now, it is because the Tristan story developed quite independently of Arthurian legends into the superb thirteenth-century German poem by Gottfried von Strassburg, *Tristan und Isolde*. Only in late French stories does Tristan become a knight of the Round Table; he never became firmly a part of the Arthurian story, and he does not fit very comfortably into Malory's book.

All this may sound as if I am trying to discourage you from reading Malory. Far from it. If you read nothing else in Malory,

read his final story, "The Tale of the Death of King Arthur."
Here Malory's voice finds its own vision. In outline the story is
very much the same as in the last part of the "Prose *Lancelot*."
The adulterous love of Launcelot and Guenever is exposed through
the plotting of Agravaine and Mordred; Arthur is forced to sentence Guenever; Launcelot, in rescuing the Queen from the stake,
accidentally kills Gawaine's brothers Gaheris and Gareth; Arthur
and Gawaine besiege Launcelot's castle; at the Pope's request,
Launcelot surrenders Guenever to Arthur and sails to his lands in
France; Gawaine, bent on revenge, persuades Arthur to lead an
army against Launcelot, and is wounded in combat with Launcelot; Mordred rebels; Gawaine dies, forgiving Launcelot; Mordred
and Arthur mortally wound each other in battle; Guenever re-
nounces Launcelot and enters a convent; Launcelot becomes a
hermit, and dies repentant.

All very similar to the earlier version, as I said—but, as Malory
tells it, very different. His version is realistic and tragic: he sees
a kingdom destroyed by human pettiness and folly, and by divided
loyalties. All of the characters are complex rather than simple.
Mordred acts originally from envy of Launcelot rather than ambition to rule the kingdom. Gawaine is loyal not to the kingdom
but to persons. He refuses to act against Launcelot throughout the
exposure of the adultery and Guenever's punishment, although
Launcelot kills several of his relatives when he is trapped with the
queen. It is the slaying of his favorite brother Gareth, which
Gawaine at first cannot believe, that drives him from friendship
to hatred. And it is Gawaine who urges Arthur into the war that
gives Mordred his chance to sieze the kingdom, as he himself at
last confesses to Arthur: "Mine uncle King Arthur, said Sir Gawaine, wit you well my death day is come, and all is through mine
own hastiness and wilfulness . . . and had Sir Launcelot been with
you as he was, this unhappy war had never begun; and of all this
am I causer." Gawaine's dying letter to Launcelot is a noble act:
"I will that all the world wit, that I, Sir Gawaine, knight of the
Table Round, sought my death, and not through thy deserving,
but it was mine own seeking."

Launcelot, for all his nobility, is torn between loyalty to king
and kingdom and love for Guenever. Both are equally strong: he
suffers because he cannot or will not choose between them until

he is forced to act against the king to save Guenever from death. He fights against Arthur reluctantly: "Alas, said Sir Launcelot, I have no heart to fight against my lord Arthur, for ever meseemeth I do not as I ought to do." He surrenders Guenever willingly when he is assured that no harm will come to her. He mourns deeply over his accidental killing of his friend Gareth and makes every effort to be reconciled with Gawaine: he wounds him only after Gawaine issues a challenge that Launcelot cannot refuse without losing his honor as a knight. On hearing of Mordred's rebellion, he sails to aid Arthur but arrives too late. His bitterest moment comes when he finds Guenever and is advised by her to return home and marry someone else. "Now, sweet madam, said Sir Launcelot, would ye that I should now return again unto my country, and there to wed a lady? Nay, madam, wit you well that shall I never do, for I shall never be so false to you of that I have promised; but the same destiny that ye have taken you to, I will take me unto, for to please Jesu, and ever for you I cast me specially to pray. For sithen ye have taken you to perfection, I must needs take me to perfection, of right. For I take record of God, in you I have had mine earthly joy; and if I had found you now so disposed, I had cast me to have had you into mine own realm."

Guenever is also divided in her loyalties. She has a genuine fondness for her husband and a concern for the kingdom; she is deeply in love with Launcelot. Like Launcelot, she cannot choose until she is condemned to death. She willingly returns to Arthur for the sake of restoring peace to the realm. And she is far more sensitive than Launcelot to the public consequences of their private acts; as we have just seen, he wishes to marry her after Arthur's death, but she refuses. "When Sir Launcelot was brought to her, then she said to all the ladies: Through this man and me hath all this war been wrought, and the death of the most noblest knights of the world; for through our love that we have loved together is my most noble lord slain. Therefore, Sir Launcelot, I require thee and beseech thee heartily, for all the love that ever was betwixt us, that thou never see me more in the visage; for as well as I have loved thee, mine heart will not serve me to see thee, for through thee and me is the flower of kings and knights destroyed." When Launcelot asks for a final kiss, "Nay, said the queen, that shall I never do, but abstain you from such works."

As for Arthur, he is more pathetic than impressive through most of the story. And he too is divided in his loyalties. When Launcelot and Guenever are accused, he insists that Agravaine and Mordred produce strong evidence. Malory informs us that "the king was full loath thereto, that any noise should be upon Sir Launcelot and his queen; for the king had a deeming, but he would not hear of it, for Sir Launcelot had done so much for him and the queen so many times, that wit ye well the king loved him passingly well." It is not only personal affection that makes Arthur reluctant to proceed against Launcelot; he is concerned with keeping the kingdom united, and only with Launcelot's aid can that be done. But as king he must take public action when Guenever is proven an adulteress: "Alas, me sore repenteth, said the king, that ever Sir Launcelot should be against me. Now I am sure the noble fellowship of the Round Table is broken forever, for with him will many a noble knight hold; and now it is fallen so, said the king, that I may not with my worship, but the queen must suffer the death."

Arthur is not sorry that Guenever is saved by Launcelot. What grieves him is the death of so many of his knights and the loss of Launcelot and his comrades: "Alas that ever this war began." He has no choice but to make war on Launcelot, but he makes his feelings very plain: "Much more I am sorrier for my good knights' loss than for the loss of my fair queen; for queens I might have enow, but such a fellowship of good knights shall never be together in no company." He is far more bitter towards Agravaine and Mordred for revealing the adultery than he is towards Launcelot for committing it; he judges the characters of the men accurately, and is more concerned for the division caused in his kingdom than for any personal grievance. Arthur speaks as he must in challenging Launcelot to battle, but there is the sense that he is simply going through the motions; it is Gawaine who speaks with fierce hatred. When Launcelot refuses a chance to kill him in battle, Arthur is so overwhelmed by his courtesy that he cannot bear to look at him; when Launcelot surrenders Guenever, all the knights except Gawaine are moved to tears, and so is Arthur. When Gawaine insists on pursuing Launcelot into France, Arthur aids his nephew against his former friend: here if anywhere he is at fault, and he moves through this part of the story like a man numb with despair, indifferent to what may happen. He recovers when Mordred rebels, becoming once more a great warrior as he drives back Mordred's knights when they try to prevent his landing in Britain. But as Gawaine is dying, Arthur says to him: "Now is my joy gone, for in Sir Launcelot and you I most had my joy; wherefore all mine earthly joy is gone from me." He is again a savage fighter in his last battle; when, after most of the knights in both armies are slain, he sees Mordred, he ignores all warnings: "Tide me death, betide me life, saith the king, now I see him yonder alone he shall never escape mine hands." In Arthur's last moments, he has the regal dignity that is lacking earlier. As Sir Bedivere grieves, "Comfort thyself, said the king, and do as well as thou mayst, for in me is no trust for to trust in; for I will unto the vale of Avilion to heal me of my grievous wound: and if thou hear never more of me, pray for my soul."

England in the fifteenth century was a nation suffering from civil warfare. Malory's power in this story comes from firsthand experience: his vision is of a kingdom destroyed not deliberately and not by any single person or action, but by the varied acts of a group of complex people, most of them willing but unable to keep the kingdom united and at peace. Nothing could be further from the conquests and the betrayal performed by the simple characters of Geoffrey of Monmouth.

*   *   *   *   *

We have been listening to medieval voices and visions. Arthurian stories continued in the sixteenth century to influence not only literature but political life. Henry Tudor based his claim to the throne of England on his supposed descent from the last British king recorded in Geoffrey of Monmouth's book, and he named his first son Arthur. This was the second attempt by a king of England to create an Arthur II. It failed when young Arthur died and Henry VIII inherited the crown. One of the best English poets of the sixteenth century, Edmund Spenser, used Arthur to represent the height of human nobility in *The Faerie Queene*. Spenser's Prince Arthur plays only a minor part in the actions of the poem, however, and while the fairyland setting and the ideals of knighthood are certainly influenced by the legendary Britain of medieval stories, there is no reason to discuss the work further. In the seventeenth century, John Milton thought for a time of writing an epic poem about Arthur. He decided against it because he wanted to base the poem on historical truth, and he became more and more doubtful that Arthur had ever existed. In the end, Milton turned to the Bible for his epic, and wrote *Paradise Lost*. An Arthurian epic *was* written in the seventeenth century, by Sir Richard Blackmore: this is such a dismal failure that there is no point in talking about it. Arthur's long reign over the European imagination seemed to be at an end.

In literature if not in life, the prophecy of Arthur's return came true. The nineteenth century's interest in medieval literature and art led naturally to a new interest in Arthur. Many Victorian authors wrote Arthurian poems, but the greatest voice and vision of the age was Alfred Lord Tennyson's, in his *Idylls of the King*.

Tennyson stated that "the vision of Arthur as I have drawn him came upon me when, little more than a boy, I first lighted upon Malory." Malory's book was the chief source of Tennyson's, and like Malory, Tennyson wrote not a single narrative but a sequence of stories. He uses Malory's general pattern: the sequence begins with "The Coming of Arthur," in which the kingdom is founded, and ends with "The Passing of Arthur" and the destruction of the kingdom; in between, there are ten poems, some of them dealing with the adventures of Arthur's knights, others with the forces that gradually undo Arthur's work. There is a greater unity than in Malory; indeed, Tennyson insisted that the total work had a central spiritual meaning. "Arthur was allegorical to me. I intended to represent him as the Ideal of the Soul of Man coming in contact with the warring elements of the flesh."

In his opening poem, Tennyson deliberately makes Arthur a remote and mysterious character. "The Coming of Arthur" is concerned mainly with Leodogran, Guinevere's father, as he considers Arthur's request to marry his daughter. We are given throughout the poem the contradictory stories of Arthur's origins as Leodogran hears them; he hears also of the arguments among the British tribal princes about accepting Arthur as their king, because of their uncertainty about his birth. Is he the son of Gorlois, Duke of Cornwall? or of Sir Anton, the old knight with whom he grew up? or of Uther, King of Britain? Leodogran finds men and women who believe one or another of these stories. Strangest of all is the story he hears from Bellicent, Uther's daughter, who reports what the magician Bleys told her as he was dying. Bleys revealed that on the night of Uther's death, Merlin and Bleys had seen

> . . . a ship, the shape thereof
> A dragon wing'd, and all from stem to stern
> Bright with a shining people on the decks,
> And gone as soon as seen. And then the two
> Dropt to the cove, and watch'd the great sea fall,
> Wave after wave, each mightier than the last,
> Till last, a ninth one, gathering half the deep
> And full of voices, slowly rose and plunged
> Roaring, and all the wave was in a flame:
> And down the wave and in the flame was borne
> A naked babe, and rode to Merlin's feet,
> Who stoopt and caught the babe, and cried, "The King!
> Here is an heir for Uther!"

But Merlin will not say whether this is the truth or not, answering only in riddles: "From the great deep to the great deep he goes."

Arthur himself is not questioned, and it is mainly through other people that we, like Leodogran, learn about him. Tennyson's meaning is clear: Arthur's right to rule must be accepted by an act of faith, not because of clear proof. There is an obvious and intentional parallel to Christ here, as in the later poems. Arthur's warriors at his coronation cry out, "Be thou the king, and we will work thy will / Who love thee"; when he speaks to them

> With large, divine, and comfortable words,
> Beyond my tongue to tell thee—I beheld
> From eye to eye through all their Order flash
> A momentary likeness of the King:
> And ere it left their faces, thro' the cross
> And those around it and the Crucified,
> Down from the casement over Arthur, smote
> Flame-colour, vert and azure, in three rays. . . .

We see Arthur directly, and hear his view of himself, only once in this first poem. When he desires to marry Guinevere, he thinks

> Shall I not lift her from this land of beasts
> Up to my throne, and side by side with me?
> What happiness to reign a lonely king . . .
> Vext with waste dreams? for saving I be join'd
> To her that is the fairest under heaven,
> I seem as nothing in the mighty world,
> And cannot will my will, nor work my work
> Wholly, nor make myself in mine own realm
> Victor and lord. But were I join'd with her,
> Then might we live together as one life,
> And reigning with one will in everything
> Have power on this dark land to lighten it,
> And power on this dead world to make it live.

So Tennyson's vision of Arthur, established in this first poem, is of a kind of messiah, a perfect man who tries to create a perfect society, and for a time succeeds. The opening poem ends with a very condensed treatment of the battles that for earlier poets had been the center of interest:

> And Arthur and his knighthood for a space
> Were all one will, and thro' that strength the King
> Drew in the petty princedoms under him,
> Fought, and in twelve great battles overcame
> The heathen hordes, and made a realm and reign'd.

In the poems that follow, Tennyson concentrates on the individual stories of Gareth and Lynette, Geraint and Enid. He attempts to make them parts of the total work by suggesting that on Gareth and Geraint the example and influence of Arthur, Lancelot, and Guinevere work to develop goodness in these knights. We catch rather distant glimpses of Arthur administering justice; he is continually referred to as "the blameless king." Throughout this group of poems, there is no evil in the relationship between Lancelot and Guinevere.

With "Balin and Balan," darkness begins to enter the work. Balin models himself on Lancelot, and in the belief that Lancelot is inspired by a pure devotion to Guinevere, devotes himself to her also. As a result, "all the world / Made music, and he felt his being move / In music with his Order, and the King." But he overhears a doubtful conversation between Lancelot and Guinevere, then is scorned by a knight for believing that the queen is chaste, then hears a lying story from Vivien about the two as lovers. Balin's faith in the ideals of Arthur's court is shattered, and the violent temper which that faith had enabled him to control breaks loose and causes him to kill and be killed by his brother Balan.

In "Merlin and Vivien," the lady is sent by King Mark of Cornwall to disrupt the court. She tries to tempt Arthur himself, but fails; Merlin, however, falls for her charms, and his wisdom is lost to Arthur when she uses a spell he has taught her and imprisons him asleep in an oak tree. During her conversation with him, she accuses most of the Knights of the Round Table of not keeping their vows; Merlin can deny everything but her accusation of Lancelot and Guinevere.

In "Lancelot and Elaine," we see more directly the relationship between the two. Lancelot's love for the queen prevents him from returning Elaine's love, and she dies; Guinevere is insanely jealous when she thinks Lancelot loves another woman. Lancelot is shown tormented by his guilt; his actions either make men worse because they follow his example or make the sin itself seem less because of his otherwise noble character: "Alas for Arthur's greatest knight, a man / Not after Arthur's heart!" While he wishes to break his tie to Guinevere, he cannot bring himself to do so: "His honour rooted in dishonour stood, / And faith unfaithful kept him falsely true."

However much Tennyson draws the basic stories in his book from Malory, the meaning he gives them is very much his own. This is particularly true of "The Holy Grail." Tennyson develops what is barely suggested in Malory and the French *Lancelot*, and turns the Grail quest into a major cause of the downfall of Arthur's kingdom. Arthur himself is not present when the Grail, "all over cover'd with a luminous cloud," appears to the knights, causing them to vow to ride in search of it. When Arthur returns and hears what has happened, he is severe in his disapproval: "Had I been here, ye had not sworn the vow." Arthur calls the Grail "a sign to maim this Order which I made"; he comments that Galahad and Percivale may be singled out for this quest, but the other knights by making the vow have deserted their responsibilities:

> . . . how often, O my knights,
> Your place being vacant at my side,
> This chance of noble deeds will come and go
> Unchallenged, while ye follow wandering fires
> Lost in the quagmire!

Guinevere cries out as the knights and especially Lancelot ride out on the quest: "This madness has come on us for our sins." And clearly Tennyson presents the Grail chiefly as a temptation to the ordinary knights whose vocation is to keep order in society, not to pursue the solitary religious life—the knights are tempted and fall as a way of punishing the court for its sins. Tennyson does keep the earlier use of the Grail quest: in pursuing it, the knights are tested, and all but Galahad, Percivale, and Bors fail to prove virtuous enough to achieve the vision of the Grail. For Lancelot in particular, the quest turns into an agonizing discovery of how greatly he has sinned. The poem ends with Arthur's assertion:

> And some among you held, that if the King
> Had seen the sight he would have sworn the vow:
> Not easily, seeing that the King must guard
> That which he rules, and is but as the hind
> To whom a space of land is given to plow,
> Who may not wander from the allotted field
> Before his work is done. . . .

He adds that after his work is over each day, he too experiences moments of vision

> . . . when he feels he cannot die,
> And knows himself no vision to himself,
> Nor the high God a vision, nor that One
> Who rose again.

The Grail quest leaves Arthur "gazing at a barren board, / And a lean Order." The following story, "Pelleas and Ettare," shows the further corruption of that Order. Gawain betrays Pelleas by taking Ettare for himself; when Pelleas hears of Guinevere's unfaithfulness to Arthur, he rides to Camelot "to lash the treasons of the Table Round," but is stopped by Lancelot. As the poem ends, both lovers are aware of tragedy to come.

To my mind, the best poem in the *Idylls* is "The Last Tournament." Here Tennyson makes the Tristram story fit into the total pattern far better than any previous writer had done. Lancelot and Guinevere's betrayal of Arthur is paralleled by Tristram and Isolt's betrayal of Mark. But there is a difference: Lancelot and Guinevere are aware of the wrong they are doing, and are tormented by their guilt; Tristram uses their love affair as an excuse for his own, but his love for Isolt has no depth, and he has lost his nobler qualities in disillusionment. Tristram calls the vows of knighthood "the wholesome madness of an hour," declaring that

> They served their use, their time; for every knight
> Believed himself a greater than himself,

And every follower eyed him as a God;
Till he, being lifted up beyond himself,
Did mightier deeds than elsewise he had done,
And so the realm was made; but then their vows—
First mainly thro' that sullying of our Queen—
Began to gall the knighthood, asking whence
Had Arthur right to bind them to himself?

Tennyson parallels the final journey of Tristram to Isolt that ends
in death with Arthur's attack on the Red Knight. The Red
Knight's court is a twisted image of Arthur's Camelot: the Knight
declares that at least he and his men are honest in their evil, in
contrast to the hypocrisy of the Knights of the Round Table. And
Arthur's knights, though they win the victory, run wild, massacre
women as well as men, and burn the castle, deaf to the king's
orders.

A most effective character in the poem is Dagonet, the Fool, who
sees Arthur as

. . . my brother fool, the king of fools!
Conceits himself as God that he can make
Figs out of thistles, silk from bristles, milk
From burning spurge, honey from hornet-combs,
And men from beasts—Long live the king of fools!

The ending of the poem is somber. We shift from Mark's savage
and cowardly striking down of Tristram to Arthur's sickened return to a Camelot where the queen's room is dark and Dagonet
clings to his feet, sobbing that he shall never make Arthur smile
again.

Arthur does not fail the world: the world fails him. Tennyson
makes this all too clear in "Guinevere." The queen has refused to
go with Lancelot to France after their affair has been exposed by
Modred, and has taken refuge in the convent at Almesbury. You
can see how Tennyson changes the story—no sentence to burning,
no rescue by Lancelot, no flight to France. Only in this poem,
late in the sequence, are we given a full view of Guinevere. The
opening poem simply presented Lancelot officially escorting Guinevere to be married, but now we learn that on the journey she fell

in love with him and found Arthur "cold, / High, self-contain'd, and passionless, not like him, / Not like my Lancelot."

Arthur comes to the convent to see Guinevere for the last time. The characterization of Guinevere is very effective, but I have my doubts about that of Arthur. Not until this poem are we given a really close look at Arthur, and I am not very happy with what I see. Arthur may have struck you already as irritatingly aware of his own superiority to other men, as extremely lacking in compassion for the weaknesses of others. That is not what Tennyson intended; he certainly meant us to see Arthur as "blameless." The trouble is that he is so very aware that he is blameless, so insistent on how Guinevere has failed to appreciate him and therefore "spoilt the purpose of my life," so full of self-pity. That Arthur should grieve bitterly for the fall of his kingdom, that he should be angry with his faithless wife, is understandable. But I know of no other Arthurian story where the king is so unbearably smug:

> I was first of all the kings who drew
> The knighthood-errant of this realm and all
> The realms together under me, their Head,
> In that fair Order of my Table Round,
> A glorious company, the flower of men,
> To serve as model for the mighty world,
> And be the fair beginning of a time. . . .
> And all this throve before I wedded thee.
>
> .   .   .   .
>
> For think not, tho' thou wouldst not love thy lord,
> Thy lord has wholly lost his love for thee.
> I am not made of so slight elements.
> Yet must I leave thee, woman, to thy shame.
>
> .   .   .   .
>
> Lo! I forgive thee, as Eternal God
> Forgives: do thou for thine own soul the rest.
>
> .   .   .   .
>
> Hereafter in that world where all are pure
> We two may meet before high God, and thou
> Wilt spring to me, and claim me thine, and know
> I am thine husband—not a smaller soul,
> Nor Lancelot, nor another.

Tennyson meant us to find Arthur entirely admirable, to see
him as Guinevere does at the end of this poem:

> I thought I could not breathe in that fine air,
> That pure severity of perfect light—
> I yearn'd for warmth and colour which I found
> In Lancelot—now I see thee what thou art,
> Thou art the highest and most human too,
> Not Lancelot, nor another.

But do we really see Arthur this way? I have more trouble en-
joying Tennyson's vision of Arthur than I do with any other
poet's, and I think the fault is not mine but his. Tennyson has
deliberately suggested that Arthur is Christ-like, attempting to lead
men to their highest possibilities but suffering betrayal by them.
But Christ—whatever one's religious beliefs are—is so much more
"human" than Arthur: calmly certain of his own virtue but never
arrogant, loving in his personal relationships, preaching and living
perfection but understanding of those who fail. The author who
tries to imagine a completely good human being sets himself an
almost impossible task, and we can sympathize with Tennyson's
difficulties. But it was his choice to present Arthur at such a dis-
tance from us through most of the *Idylls*. We can understand why
Guinevere found him "cold"; it is harder to understand why at the
end she thinks him "highest and most human too."

In his final poem, "The Passing of Arthur," Tennyson attempts
to give Arthur added humanity by showing him in torment before
his last battle. There is an obvious parallel to Christ's agony in the
garden.

> I found Him in the shining of the stars,
> I mark'd Him in the flowering of His fields,
> But in His ways with men I find Him not.
> I waged His wars, and now I pass and die.
> O me! for why is all around us here
> As if some lesser god had made the world,
> But had not force to shape it as he would,
> Till the High God behold it from beyond,
> And enter it, and make it beautiful?

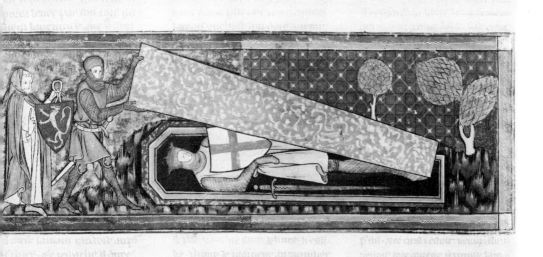

Arthur can at last admit the possibility of a flaw in himself, though
the flaw is limited to not understanding God's total purpose in His
dealings with men. He still does not blame himself for anything
that has happened; he almost despairs, however, in words that echo
Christ's:

> For I, being simple, thought to work His will,
> And have but stricken with the sword in vain;
> And all whereon I lean'd in wife and friend
> Is traitor to my peace, and all my realm
> Reels back into the beast, and is no more.
> My God, thou hast forgotten me in my death:
> Nay—God my Christ—I pass but shall not die.

Tennyson, as the last line shows, keeps the mystery of Arthur in
this final poem, though this presents a problem. For Arthur to be a

mystery to his people or to us can be effective, but should he be a mystery to himself? "I perish by this people which I made,— / Tho' Merlin swore that I should come again / To rule once more; but, let what will be, be." Taken by itself, "The Passing of Arthur" does succeed in humanizing the hero of the *Idylls* at last, in his nightmare-like experience of the battle, his doubts, his longing for the golden times of Camelot and his grief for the knights he loved. His final speech to Bedivere shows quiet resignation, hope, and even humility:

> The old order changeth, yielding place to new,
> And God fulfills Himself in many ways,
> Lest one good custom should corrupt the world.
> Comfort thyself: what comfort is in me?
> I have lived my life, and that which I have done
> May He within Himself make pure!

Whatever faults one finds in the work, Tennyson's poetic power made his vision of Arthur and his Britain popular in his own century and in ours. Certainly his influence has been as strong as Malory's on later versions of the story. It has influenced some writers in a negative way: they have presented visions of Arthur as unlike Tennyson's as possible.

*   *   *   *   *

There have been many retellings of Arthur's story in the twentieth century. One of the best-known is T. H. White's *The Once and Future King,* on which the stage and film musical *Camelot* was based. It may surprise you that I am not going to pay much attention to this version of the story. But I have my reasons.

White, in my view, fails to mix comedy and tragedy successfully in the later and most important part of the story, and the result leaves me very much unsatisfied with the book. I am willing to admit that there are fine moments: one of the best is Arthur's scene before the last battle, in which he broods despairingly about violence, "the mental illness of humanity," and talks with his young page boy. The boy is the future Sir Thomas Malory—and that brings me to my second reason. White admits his debt to Malory, saying that "almost all the people in this book are in his wonderful one, *and have the same characters in both.*" So, despite White's original touches, I cannot see that his vision of Arthur's Britain does more than repeat Malory's, with a few bits derived from Tennyson.

I had better add that my doubts about White do not apply to the first of his Arthurian stories, *The Sword in the Stone*. (But please read this as White first published it; he changed the story when it was included in *The Once and Future King*, and the changes spoil it.) *The Sword in the Stone* is a delightful treatment of Arthur's boyhood. White creates a comic and sometimes beautiful fantasy world, complete with a Merlin who wears tennis shorts and explains: "I unfortunately was born at the wrong end of time, and I have to live *backwards* from in front, while surrounded by a lot of people living forwards from behind." It is no great surprise that Robin Hood comes into the story, leaning on his bow with a "look of negligent woodcraft." It is *that* kind of story, set in "the old Merry England when the rosy barons ate with their fingers, and had peacocks served before them with all their tail feathers streaming, or boars' heads with the tusks stuck in again; when there was no unemployment because there were too few people to be unemployed; when the forests rang with knights walloping each other on the helm, and the unicorns in the wintry moonlight stamped with their silver feet and snorted their noble breaths of blue upon the frozen air." And most marvellous of all, in this fairy tale England, "the weather behaved itself"!

I want to turn now, though, to the two modern retellings of Arthur's story that I find truly outstanding. They could hardly be more different—one is a series of very difficult poems; the other is an historical novel.

Charles Williams died in 1945 before he had completed the Arthurian poems begun in *Taliessin through Logres* and *The Region of the Summer Stars*. Several of the most important poems had not been written, and Williams had not yet placed the separate poems in their final order. Fortunately he had written a prose study of the Arthurian legend, "The Figure of Arthur," and his close friend C. S. Lewis published this, together with a very helpful commentary on the poems, in *Arthurian Torso*. So we have some notion of what the sequence of the poems would have been. Williams' vision of Arthur is completely and deliberately the opposite of Tennyson's. He observed that for many writers, including Tennyson, the Grail was only an episode in the story. For Williams, the Grail is central to the story. He does not see it as a temptation, as Tennyson did, or a testing, as some medieval writers did: he sees it as a divinely ordained opportunity. Arthur's Britain exists so that the Grail may come and bless mankind.

Williams borrows a Welsh word and calls Arthur's Britain "Logres." He imagines it as a province of the Empire; he sees the Empire itself as resembling the human body, and both body and Empire are called to become "the Kingdom of God." Because Logres is the "head" of the Empire, it is through Logres that the Grail is destined to come to man. But that is not exactly Williams' way of seeing it: the Grail will offer itself to Logres, allowing man to achieve the joy of fulfillment. Unlike in Tennyson, the Grail in Williams is not for a select few: it is meant for all men. The fulfillment it brings is not for man's spirit alone; in Williams' vision, flesh and spirit are called to union, harmony, and joy. And man's most serious faults are of the spirit rather than of the flesh. In all of these ways, then, Williams' vision of Arthur's Britain is in marked contrast to Tennyson's.

Williams' vision of Arthur's Britain is of another Fall of Man, another Paradise Lost. Logres can only achieve the Grail and begin to be part of the Kingdom of God if its leaders can give themselves to what is greater than themselves. And this they fail to do. Tennyson entitled his poem of the founding of the kingdom "The Coming of Arthur"; Williams entitles his parallel poem "The Calling of Arthur." Williams' Arthur is not a blameless messiah figure who comes to bring men to his own higher level; he is a man called by God to make Logres ready for the Grail, and we see him at his coronation already asking the question which he will answer wrongly: "The king made for the kingdom, or the kingdom made for the king?" Into the general subject of Logres' being worthy of receiving the Grail when it is offered, Williams fits other stories that had become part of Arthurian legend: the incest in which Mordred was conceived, the killing of Balan by Balin, the affair of Guinevere and Lancelot. In Williams, what is wrong with the relationship of Guinevere and Lancelot is similar to Arthur's fault. As Arthur selfishly sees the kingdom as existing for himself, so Lancelot and Guinevere see love as existing for their own satisfactions. Their love is not evil in itself: if they had given themselves fully to the right order of love, they would have sacrificed the

satisfaction of the flesh, won a richer fulfillment, and helped pre-
pare Logres for the Grail. But romantic love and social order both
become warped and finally blank, meaningless. At Mass, Arthur
worships the image of himself as king; Lancelot adores the Queen.
The Grail when it comes cannot be achieved by all Logres, the
earthly society does not become the Kingdom of God, and Logres,
divided not united, fades into the imperfect Britain of imperfect
men.

Not all is lost. The Grail is achieved by a few, Galahad, Percivale, Bors. The Company founded by the court bard Taliessin attempts to live the self-sacrificing life of joy that all Logres should
have lived, and so offers a continuing opportunity for joy to other
men. The sequence ends in a redemptive vision as Lancelot, now a
priest, says Mass. The hope for achieving the Kingdom of God
remains, even though the Empire itself falls apart, and Logres becomes "mere Britain."

I find Williams' vision of Arthur and his Britain more satisfying
in its unity and depth of meaning than that of any other Arthurian
poet. But the words I have borrowed from Williams for this book
are true of his own poetry: "more than the voice is the vision."
Williams' poetic voice can be powerful, sometimes beautiful, sometimes harshly dramatic. Sarras, the glorious city to which Galahad
is called, is described as

> . . . a clear city on a sea-site
> in a light that shone from beyond the sun.

"The Calling of Arthur" ends in a rush of compressed action followed by one quiet but weighty line:

> Arthur ran; the people marched: in the snow
> King Cradlemas died in his litter; a screaming few
> fled; Merlin came; Camelot grew.
> In Logres the king's friend landed, Lancelot of Gaul.

Mordred, as he plans to seize the kingdom, sums himself up in a
single, hushed, terrifying line: "I will sit here alone." But only at
moments can Williams' voice express his vision adequately: too
often he creates difficulties by obscure references and by strained

compressed lines where words carry meanings known only to Williams. His vision is steady; his voice often falters in the effort to give it expression.

It is too early to know whether the "Arthuriad," as Lewis calls it, will live as Malory and Tennyson still live. If it does, it will be less because of Williams' poetic skill than because of his powerful vision. And that is how Williams himself would have wanted it.

The Poet as a teller of tales usually asks us to read his work only as fiction, as make-believe. But when the Poet takes the role of a historical novelist, he says to us: "This is the way things really may have happened." The historical novelist not only must satisfy us by the shape of the story and the behavior of the characters, but he must also meet the standards we normally apply to the Historian. It does not trouble us in Williams or in Tennyson or in earlier writers if Arthur's court belongs more to the twelfth century than to the sixth, or if it is a golden court that could exist only in a story; it does not trouble us that characters of other stories and times, Lancelot and Merlin, Percival and Galahad, are part of Arthur's world. But a historical novelist, though he is allowed to make up stories and characters, must give us a possible Arthur in a convincing sixth-century Britain. George Finkel, for example, in a generally good novel, *Watch-Fires to the North*, succeeds in creating a vivid picture of Britain in Arthur's time. I do not agree with Finkel's version of what happened, but most of it is at least possible. What bothers me is that he keeps trying to put characters from later legends into the historical setting—Galahad, for instance. I keep saying as I read, "That just could not have happened." I cannot simply relax and enjoy the story.

It is otherwise with Rosemary Sutcliff's *Sword at Sunset*. Here is a vision of Arthur based firmly on historical research; while I may not agree entirely with her interpretations, she imagines fully believable and fascinating characters in a strongly realistic Dark Age Britain. Her preface states her view of Arthur, and her purpose in the novel:

> No knight in shining armor, no Round Table, no many-towered Camelot; but a Romano-British war-leader, to whom, when the Barbarian darkness came flooding in, the last guttering lights of civilization seemed worth fighting for. *Sword at Sunset* is an attempt

to re-create from fragments of known facts, from likelihoods and deductions and guesswork pure and simple, the kind of man this war-leader may have been, and the story of his long struggle.

While I was writing the first part of this book, I often envied Miss Sutcliff her freedom to invent incidents where history has only blank spaces. And I had to be very careful not to be influenced by Miss Sutcliff's powerful imagination in making my own reconstruction of events.

Sword at Sunset uses from the legends of Arthur "the original framework, or rather two interwrought frameworks: the Sin [incest] which carries with it its own retribution; the Brotherhood broken by the love between the leader's woman and his closest friend. These have the inevitability and pitiless purity of outline that one finds in classical tragedy, and that belong to the ancient and innermost places of man." As a novelist, she has the right to do this; as a historical novelist, she manages the framework so that it can be accepted as possible for these people at this moment in time. Guenhumara's lover is not Lancelot, whom the author rightly calls a "later French importation," but Bedwyr, who was probably one of Arthur's real comrades.

Miss Sutcliff is correct in claiming that "almost every part of the story, even to the unlikely linkup between Medraut and that mysterious Saxon with a British name, Cerdic the half-legendary founder of Wessex, has some kind of basis outside the author's imagination." But, without that imagination, historical accuracy would not have been enough. Miss Sutcliff's realistic vision of Arthur lives because she is, above all, a fine novelist.

*   *   *   *   *

We began this look at Arthurian literature with Geoffrey of Monmouth in 1136; we end with Rosemary Sutcliff in 1963. You may find, as I do, an odd kind of pleasure in discovering that, after eight hundred years of varied voices and visions, we have come from a work of history that is really fiction to a work of fiction that is truly historical.

6

The Vision of the Kingdom

In this final chapter, as I said at the beginning of the book, the Historian confronts the Poet. I had better make a few things clear, however. The Poet has the right to use Arthur's Britain as he pleases to express a meaningful vision, and we have seen a number of poets doing exactly that. As long as the Poet is simply creating a fictional world, the Historian has no right to object. He can be curious, though, about the Poet's vision. Without fussing about the details of historical setting and plot, are there some basic truths about Arthur and his Britain that the Poet has been able to capture and express? Can the Historian use the Poet's vision to see more clearly what Arthur really accomplished? Or are the Poet's and the Historian's visions of the kingdom completely at odds?

The Poet has always seen a pattern in Arthur's story, even though individual poets differ about incidents, characters, and meaning. That pattern can be outlined as follows: (1) The Triumph, (2) The Reign, (3) The Betrayal, (4) The Hope. This pattern is what the Historian must explore.

The Triumph of Arthur has been a part, often the major part, of every poet's vision. The nature of the Triumph varies from poet to poet: Geoffrey, as we saw, claims most of Europe for Arthur, and many poets follow Geoffrey in this; other poets, such as Tennyson and even the very visionary Williams, limit the Triumph to Britain. The Historian, after being doubtful for centuries, now finds the Poet's vision essentially true. Every scholar of early British history now agrees that there was a major victory over the Anglo-Saxons. But some historians are still doubtful about giving Arthur credit for

the Triumph. You know my opinion; it is only fair to let you hear
a few cautious or dissenting voices—Kenneth Jackson's, for instance:

> There may have been a supreme British commander of genius in the
> late fifth century who bore the Roman-derived name of Arthur,
> though it would be wrong to deduce anything about his background
> from his name. There is little reason to think that he held any definite
> sub-Roman office, whether *Dux Bellorum* or otherwise, and his
> supposed cavalry tactics are an illusion.

Jackson is cautious and rather negative. Nora K. Chadwick is far
more negative: "The present writer is of the opinion that we
might regard him as a member of the ruling dynasty of Argyll
[Dalriata], which seems to have had strong British ties by intermarriage." Mrs. Charwick favors an Arthur who fought only in
the north; T. C. Lethbridge also believes in an Arthur who fought
"long after the main settlement of the Saxons was complete," but
in defense of south Wales, not northern Britain. If after this you
want to be reassured, other equally respected historians, such as
John R. Morris, are convinced that the Triumph was Arthur's and
that the version of it I have given you is not only possible but
probable.

As for Arthur's Reign, the Poet has difficulties envisioning it
that are of particular interest to the Historian. The Poet sees it
generally as a kind of Golden Age, a period of social harmony and
high civilization. The Historian notes that those poets who do not
pass quickly over the Reign, who attempt to treat it in some detail,
shift their attention from Arthur himself to the deeds of individual
knights. While the Historian must regard these deeds as fictional, he
does find a kind of symbolic quality in this treatment: only the ab-
sence of warfare on a large scale permits the individual characters'
smaller experiences to become of central interest. For the Historian,
the period of the Reign is almost blank. That the Poet, who is
happiest when he can deal with exciting incidents, avoids the
difficulties of imagining the details of Arthur's administration is
therefore a help to the Historian. It shows him how the human
imagination works: the blank record is exactly what the Historian
would expect to find if the Reign really was an age of constant,
undramatic labor to build and preserve a good society. Layamon's

statement that "the king held all his people together in great happiness" draws from the Historian not argument but general agreement.

The major event that became part of the Poet's vision of the Reign, the Grail Quest, must, of course, be regarded as fiction by the Historian. That does not mean he dismisses it as of no value to him. He finds instead that this too has a symbolic quality. The Reign was in fact, his evidence shows, a time when British Christianity flourished, especially in the form of monastic life. The personal search for sanctity and the social effort to make the kingdom a Christian community really happened in Arthur's Britain.

The Poet's vision of the Betrayal begins with a personal as well as a political unfaithfulness to Arthur on the part of his nephew Modred. As we have seen, this simple enough beginning grew into a much more complicated pattern of betrayals: Guenevere, at first a passive victim forced to marry Modred, is joined by Lancelot in a personal betrayal of Arthur that becomes, against their wills, a political betrayal as well; Modred becomes not simply Arthur's nephew but also his illegitimate son, the product of Arthur's lust and incest. What is the Historian's view of this? He has no evidence that will let him accept any of it as true, except for Modred's rebellion. He does find, however, that the vision once more gives a symbol of what was historically true. Arthur's Britain was destroyed not by outside enemies but by internal conflicts. The sober voice of a historian, R. H. Hodgkin, sums it up very well: "If the Romano-Britons could only have organized a united front, the future might have lain with them, and Britain might never have given place to England."

The last part of the Poet's vision, the Hope of Arthur's survival and return, you may expect the Historian to call merely wishful thinking by the defeated Celts. But the Historian does not find it that simple. Of course he cannot accept, any more than certain poets could, an Arthur who did not really die. The Historian sees, however, that, though Arthur's Britain as an actual kingdom perished, it lived on as an idea, in ways that Arthur himself could not have foreseen.

It would not have surprised Arthur that the dream of a Britain freed from English rule survived for centuries among the Welsh. Nor would he have been surprised that Wales could unite only for brief periods during those centuries, and finally lost its independence in 1282 because of tribal struggles. The vision is far from dead, though: the Welsh Nationalist Party, *Plaid Cymru*, is politically stronger right now than it has ever been.

What would certainly have surprised Arthur is that his ideal of a united Britain proved to be stronger among the Saxons than among the Britons. The Saxons went through centuries of their own tribal struggles, but the Saxon term *Bretwalda*, ruler of Britain, passed as a more and more meaningful title from one English king to another, until in 829 Egbert of Wessex became acknowledged ruler of all Britain. There were later complications, but the political unity of the kingdom had been achieved, and it was never lost for long. It was that unity, strengthened under Norman rulers, that caused the defeat of the divided Britons of Wales.

Arthur's Britain had meant more than political unity, important as this was. It was a kingdom of the mind and the spirit, and this too lived on. The British failure to convert and instruct the Saxons was redeemed by the Irish monks who carried on and developed the British monastic traditions. The sixth-century Irish monastery at Clonard was modeled on the British examples: its abbot Finnian was later called "the teacher of the saints of Ireland." His students both founded their own monasteries and influenced others to follow their example. Colum Cille, the best known of Finnian's disciples, established a famous monastic community on the northwestern British island of Iona. It was on Iona that the Saxon Oswald, king of Northumbria, became a Christian. It was from Iona that Aidan came in 634, at Oswald's request, to found a monastic community on the island of Lindisfarne, not far from the king's court at Bamburgh. In the next twenty years, Aidan and his disciples firmly established Christianity in Northumbria. From this base in the north, missionaries left to preach and found monasteries in the kingdoms of Mercia and Essex. The Irish had come to the English; the English in turn went to the Irish. Young English monks were welcomed at the Irish schools, where they were provided with books and teachers.

You may have heard of Augustine's mission to Kent rather than Aidan's to Northumbria. The fact is that though Augustine and his disciple Paulinus, sent from Rome, had some success in the southeast, credit for the conversion and teaching of the Anglo-

Map 6
ANGLO-SAXON BRITAIN, ca. A.D. 700

Saxons must go chiefly to the Irish monks. Aldhelm, an extraordinary scholar of the late seventh century, was a member of the Wessex royal family who studied at Malmesbury under its Irish founder Maildubh and eventually became its abbot. Benedict Biscop, of a noble Northumbrian family, founded the monasteries of Wearmouth and Jarrow. In the tradition that had passed from Gaul to Britain, from Britain to Ireland, from Ireland to England, these were centers of learning as well as of religion. Benedict pursued this goal with special energy, making three trips to Rome to acquire books for the monastic library. Jarrow was the monastery of the famous Bede (671–735), who speaks for many men of his century and the next when he writes, quite simply, "I always took pleasure in learning, in teaching, and in writing."

Anglo-Saxon England joined Ireland in teaching western Europe during the seventh and eighth centuries. When Charlemagne, for example, wanted a teacher for his palace school, it was to England that he looked. After 782, the brilliant Alcuin of York, with many of his English students, not only taught at the Frankish court but made the abbey of St. Martin of Tours one of Europe's great centers of learning. It is a curious circle that the Historian traces—the traditions of liberal education passing from Roman Gaul through Celtic and Anglo-Saxon monasteries to the new "Roman Empire" of Charlemagne the Frank.

You may think we have wandered far from Arthur, but we have not. Consider, for a moment, the greatest Anglo-Saxon poem, *Beowulf*. It is probable that this was composed about 725 by a Northumbrian poet. It could not have been recorded if the monks of Lindisfarne had not taught their students the art of writing. It would not even have been composed, or at least it would have been a very different sort of poem, if those monks had not brought to Northumbria the respect for the nobility of pre-Christian heroic legends that was a special mark of Celtic monasticism. It is a strange thought that if Arthur, who was to become a legend himself, had not lived, we might never have heard of the legendary Beowulf.

*   *   *   *   *

For centuries, the Historian left the vision of Arthur's Britain to the Poet. Now he is developing his own vision of the kingdom and the King. The Dark Ages are still dark, but the Historian is beginning to see more clearly. For one thing, Arthur's Britain really did exist. For another, Arthur's victory at Mount Badon did more than delay the conquest of Britain by fifty years. If that battle had been lost, if the Saxons had destroyed the schools and churches in western Britain as they did in the east, there could have been no development of British learning, no voyages of Irish monks to British monasteries, no Irish mission to the Saxons.

The Historian has no way of knowing what might have happened. But he has begun to have a vision of what did happen. He is beginning to see that the history not only of England but of Europe took the course it did because of Arthur and his Britain.

Chronology

207	Romans regain control of northern Britain.
208–11	Severus defeats Picts, dies at York. Hadrian's Wall refortified.
210	Beginnings of Saxon raids on southeastern coast.
214	Emperor Caracalla confers citizenship on all free subjects of the empire.
275	Irish raids begin on southwest coast.
280	Increased Saxon raids on southeast coast.
286–93	Carausius proclaims self emperor of Britain, begins program of coastal defence.
293–96	Carausius murdered by Allectus. Northern tribes revolt. Constantius Chlorus defeats Allectus, subdues revolt, refortifies Hadrian's Wall.
306	Constantius defeats Picts, dies at York. Constantine proclaimed emperor by army in Britain.
310	Establishment of civil office, Vicar of Britain, and two military offices, Duke of Britain and Count of the Saxon Shore.
313	Constantine issues Edict of Milan, giving Christians freedom of worship.
367	Combined assault on Britain by Picts, Irish, and Saxons. Near collapse of Roman government in Britain.
368	Theodosius restores order in Britain, establishes northern treaty-kingdoms.
370	Martin of Tours becomes first monastic bishop in Gaul.
383–88	Magnus Maximus proclaimed emperor in Britain, invades Continent with British troops, is defeated by Theodosius I.
396	Stilicho sends expedition to defend Britain against Picts, Irish, and Saxons.
401	Stilicho withdraws British troops for war with Goths, creates office of Count of Britain.
406–11	Constantine III claims imperial throne, leads British troops to Continent, is defeated by Honorius. Vandals invade Gaul.
410	Visigoths under Alaric take Rome, begin invasion of southern Gaul. British told by Honorius to defend themselves.
425–30	Council of Britain, under Vortigern, establishes treaty-kingdoms of Dyfed, Gwynedd, and Ceredigion, settles Saxons along east coast. Irish establish kingdom of Dalriata.
432	Patrick begins mission to Ireland.
442	Beginning of Saxon revolt and expansion.

446	Britons plead for help from Rome, without success.
453–57	Intense Saxon raids in south. British migrations to Brittany.
460	Ambrosius becomes leader of the British.
	Birth of Arthur.
460–90	Constant warfare between Britons and Saxons. British re-occupation of hill forts, building of Wansdyke and Bokerley Dyke.
485–95	Arthur as Count of Britain, defeats Saxons and Picts in series of battles. Decisive victory at Mount Badon against Saxons.
486	Clovis I establishes Frankish kingdom in Gaul.
495–520	Arthur as emperor of Britain until death at battle of Camlann.
	Flourishing of British monasticism under leadership of Illtud.
540	Gildas writes *De Excidio Britanniae*.
550–600	Saxon conquest of Britain.
565	Colum Cille founds monastery at Iona.
634	Aidan founds monastery at Lindisfarne, begins conversion of Northumbria.

Bibliography

The following are the books, and a few articles, I consulted in writing this book. I am indebted even to those I disagree with, but I alone am responsible for the opinions expressed in this work.

I should note here that I used the translations from Anglo-Saxon poetry by Kevin Crossley-Holland and from *Sir Gawain and the Green Knight* by Brian Stone in Chapter 5. All other translations are my own, though I often followed the guidance of previous translators.

ABRAHAMS, PETER. "The Blacks." In *An African Treasury*. Edited by LANG-STON HUGHES. New York: Crown, 1960.
ASHE, GEOFFREY. *From Caesar to Arthur*. London: Collins, 1960.
———. *The Quest for Arthur's Britain*. New York: Praeger, 1968.
BEDE. *History of the English Church*. Translated by Leo Sherley-Price. Harmondsworth: Penguin, 1955.
BIRLEY, ANTHONY. *Life in Roman Britain*. New York: Putnam, 1964.
BLAIR, PETER HUNTER. *Roman Britain and Early England*. New York: Norton, 1966.
BRENGLE, RICHARD L., ed. *Arthur, King of Britain*. New York: Appleton-Century-Crofts, 1964.
BURN, A. R. *Agricola and Roman Britain*. London: Hutchinson, 1953.
CHADWICK, NORA K. *The Age of the Saints in the Early Celtic Church*. London: Oxford University Press, 1961.
———. *Celtic Britain*. New York: Praeger, 1963.
———. *Poetry and Letters in Early Christian Gaul*. London: Bowes and Bowes, 1955.
———, ed. *Studies in Early British History*. Cambridge: Cambridge University Press, 1954.
CHAMBERS, E. K. *Arthur of Britain*. London: Sidgwick and Jackson, 1927.
CHARLESWORTH, M. P. *The Lost Province*. Cardiff: University of Wales Press, 1949.

CHRÉTIEN DE TROYES. *Arthurian Romances*. Translated by W. W. COMFORT. New York: Dutton, 1914.

CLANCY, JOSEPH P., trans. *The Earliest Welsh Poetry*. New York: St. Martin's, 1970.

COLLINGWOOD, R. G., and MYRES, J. N. L. *Roman Britain and the English Settlements*. London: Oxford University Press, 1937.

COPLEY, GORDON J. *The Conquest of Wessex in the Sixth Century*. London: Phoenix House, 1954.

COTTRELL, LEONARD. *The Great Invasion*. New York: Coward-McCann, 1962.

CROSSLEY-HOLLAND, KEVIN, trans. *The Battle of Maldon*. New York: St. Martin's, 1965.

————, trans. *Beowulf*. New York: Farrar, Straus, 1968.

DILLON, MYLES, and CHADWICK, NORA K. *The Celtic Realms*. New York: New American Library, 1967.

DONAHUE, CHARLES. "*Beowulf* and Christian Tradition: A Reconsideration from a Celtic Stance." *Traditio* (1965), XXI, pp. 55-116.

DUDLEY, DONALD R., and WEBSTER, GRAHAM. *The Roman Conquest of Britain*. Chester Springs, Pa.: Dufour, 1965.

EADIE, JOHN W. "The Development of Roman Mailed Cavalry." *Journal of Roman Studies* (1967), LVII, pp. 161-167.

FRERE, SHEPPARD. *Britannia*. London: Routledge and Kegan Baul, 1967.

GEOFFREY OF MONMOUTH. *History of the Kings of Britain*. Edited and translated by LEWIS THORPE. Harmondsworth: Penguin, 1966.

HANSON, R. P. C. *Saint Patrick*. London: Oxford University Press, 1968.

HARDEN, D. B., ed. *Dark Age Britain*. London: Methuen, 1956.

H. M. Ordnance Survey. *Britain in the Dark Ages* (Map). 1966.

————. *Roman Britain* (Map). 1956.

————. *Southern Britain in the Iron Age* (Map). 1962.

HODGKIN, R. H. *A History of the Anglo-Saxons*. Oxford: Clarendon Press, 1935.

JARRETT, M. G., and DOBSON, B. eds. *Britain and Rome*. Durham: Titus Wilson, 1965.

LAYAMON. "Brut." In *Arthurian Chronicles*. Translated by EUGENE MASON. London: Dent, 1912.

LETHBRIDGE, T. C. *Merlin's Island*. London: Methuen, 1948.

————. *The Painted Men*. New York: Philosophical Library, 1954.

LINDSAY, JACK. *Arthur and His Times*. London: Muller, 1958.

LIVERSIDGE, JOAN. *Britain in the Roman Empire*. New York: Praeger, 1968.

LOOMIS, R. S., ed. *Arthurian Literature in the Middle Ages*. Oxford: Clarendon Press, 1959.

LOOMIS, R. S., and WILLARD, RUDOLPH, eds. *Medieval English Verse and Prose*. New York: Appleton-Century-Crofts, 1948.

MALORY, THOMAS. *King Arthur and His Knights*. Edited by EUGENE VINAVER. New York: Houghton Mifflin, 1969.

MILLER, HELEN HILL. *The Realms of Arthur*. New York: Scribners, 1969.

MOODY, T. W., and MARTIN, F. X., eds. *The Course of Irish History*. New York: Weybright and Talley, 1967.

MORRIS, JOHN R. *The Age of Arthur*.

PRIESTLEY, H. E. *Britain Under the Romans*. New York: Warne, 1967.

QUENNELL, MARJORIE, and QUENNELL, C. H. B. *Everyday Life in Roman and Anglo-Saxon Times.* New York: Putnam, 1959.

REES, WILLIAM. *An Historical Atlas of Wales.* London: Faber, 1959.

RICHMOND, I. A. *Roman Britain.* Harmondsworth: Penguin, 1955.

RIVET, A. L. F., ed. *The Roman Villa in Britain.* New York: Praeger, 1969.

SAKLATVALA, BERAM. *Arthur: Roman Britain's Last Champion.* New York: Taplinger, 1967.

SALWAY, PETER. *The Frontier People of Roman Britain.* Cambridge: Cambridge University Press, 1965.

SELLMAN, R. R. *The Anglo-Saxons.* New York: Roy, n.d.

———. *Roman Britain.* New York: Roy, 1956.

STENTON, F. M. *Anglo-Saxon England.* London: Oxford University Press, 1943.

STONE, B., trans. *Sir Gawain and the Green Knight.* Harmondsworth: Penguin, 1959.

SUTCLIFF, ROSEMARY. *Sword at Sunset.* New York: Coward-McCann, 1963.

TACITUS. *The Annals.* Translated by MICHAEL GRANT. Harmondsworth: Penguin, 1964.

———. *The Histories.* Translated by KENNETH WELLESLEY. Harmondsworth: Penguin, 1964.

———. *On Britain and Germany.* Translated by HAROLD MATTINGLEY. Harmondsworth: Penguin, 1948.

TENNYSON, ALFRED, Lord. *Idylls of the King.* Edited by H. H. LEVISOHN. New York: Washington Square Press, 1965.

WACE. "Roman de Brut." In *Arthurian Chronicles.* Translated by EUGENE MASON. London: Dent, 1912.

WADE-EVANS, A. W., ed. and trans. *Nennius' History of the Britons.* London: Church History Society, 1938.

WELCH, GEORGE PATRICK. *Britannia.* Middletown, Conn.: Wesleyan University Press, 1963.

WHITE, T. H. *The Once and Future King.* New York: Putnam, 1958.

———. *The Sword in the Stone.* New York: Putnam, 1939.

WHITELOCK, DOROTHY, et al., eds. and trans. *The Anglo-Saxon Chronicle.* New Brunswick: Rutgers University Press, 1962.

WILLIAMS, A. H. *An Introduction to the History of Wales.* Cardiff: University of Wales Press, 1962.

WILLIAMS, CHARLES. *Taliessin through Logres and The Region of the Summer Stars.* London: Oxford University Press, 1954.

WILLIAMS, CHARLES, and LEWIS, C. S. *Arthurian Torso.* London: Oxford University Press, 1948.

WILLIAMS, HUGH. *Christianity in Early Britain.* Oxford: Clarendon Press, 1912.

———, ed. and trans. *Gildas.* London: Cymmrodorion Society, 1901.

WOLFRAM VON ESCHENBACH. *Parzival.* Translated by HELEN M. MUSTARD and CHARLES E. PASSAGE. New York: Random House, 1961.

Index

This index lists the more important persons and places referred to in the book. Neither Arthur nor Britain is listed, because references to both occur on almost every page; the Roman Empire is not listed either, because references to it occur throughout the first half of the book.